THE BACK OF BEYOND

THE VENGEANCE OF LIP-HI-SEE

The **DANCING TUATARA PRESS**
Books from **RAMBLE HOUSE**

CLASSICS OF HORROR

CLASSICS OF SCIENCE FICTION AND FANTASY

DAY KEENE IN THE DETECTIVE PULPS

THE BACK OF BEYOND

THE VENGEANCE OF LIP-HI-SEE

Edmund Snell

Introduction by

John Pelan

RAMBLE HOUSE

Written: 1936

Introduction: © 2013 by John Pelan

Cover Design: Gavin L. O'Keefe

Preparation: Fender Tucker

ISBN 13: 978-1-60543-758-3

Dancing Tuatara Press #50

THE BACK OF BEYOND

Edmund Snell's Heart of Darkness

One comes to Dancing Tuatara Press or Ramble House Publishers to find unusual books and whether they be the lunatic webworks of Harry Stephen Keeler, the rare science fiction published under Dick Lupoff's Surinam Turtle Press or the oddball British thrillers and weird menace tales here at Dancing Tuatara Press, the one constant is that the mundane and routine is eschewed in favor of the esoteric and unusual. Accordingly, the book that you hold in your hands is one of the most unusual that it's been my privilege to introduce.

Edmund Snell is by any standard that one wants to apply, a Ramble House author, in fact, if you were to ask me to name a *typical* author in this sanctuary of the atypical, Snell would be one of the first examples that comes to mind, for he fits a lot of the criteria that one tends to associate with our books. First and foremost, he wrote "thrillers", that wonderful anything goes genre that existed before "mystery", "horror", "science fiction" and so on became marketing categories and books wherein these genres seamlessly melded together were the norm and not the exception. With Edmund Snell you never knew exactly what you were going to get. You might find supernatural horror such as *The White*

Owl, straight-forward gangster action, bizarre science fiction such as *Kontrol* or *The Sound Machine* or murder and mayhem in exotic locales (something that the well-traveled author was superbly equipped to write about.) What you probably wouldn't expect is a novel that merits comparison with Conrad's *Heart of Darkness,* a novel that has been almost completely overlooked or even misidentified as a short story collection for the last seventy-some years!

The Back of Beyond may very well be Edmund Snell's finest work, and that's high praise indeed when one considers his phenomenal output during the 1920s and 1930s. It almost seems as though there were a mandate that every general fiction magazine or story paper in the U.K. had to feature an Edmund Snell piece at least once every ninety days. This is hyperbole, of course, but for at least a twenty year stretch Snell was seemingly *everywhere,* and as mentioned previously, most of his work was of the sort that Graham Greene would call "entertainments". However, using Mr. Greene as an example, it is certainly possible for an "entertainment" to be much more than that; and that's what we have here with Mr. Snell's *The Back of Beyond.*

Readers familiar with Edmund Snell through his tales of Borneo and Singapore such as are collected in *The Finger of Destiny and Other Stories* and elsewhere know what a sure hand he had for depictions of life in the Far East. What is also clear is that Snell had little sympathy for British colonialism and had seen first-hand the evils of the Empire's expansion. *The Back of Beyond* is not only a powerful story of the darkness that can dwell within the human heart, but also a ringing denunciation of colonialism. Is *The Back of Beyond* a supernatural novel? Perhaps. Is it one of the finest and darkest novels of its type suitable to stand alongside classics such as *Blood Meridian*, *The Cross of Carl*, *Johnny Got His Gun* and *Heart of Darkness*? Absolutely. Was Edmund Snell more than just a writer of "thrillers"? We offer this book as exhibit "A".

John Pelan
Gallup, NM
2013

I. IT'S A SMALL WORLD

I

IN THE EARLY DAYS of the rubber boom, when all the world went mad, when clever paupers became wealthy men, and foolish middle-class investors became paupers, Arthur Bently and George Hansard purchased a small patch of virgin jungle in Borneo, cleared it, enduring great hardships because of lack of capital, and therefore shortage of labour, and, having planted it, waited for the trees to grow, dreaming of the time, four years or so in the future, when latex would pour from the rubber trees and money into their pockets. Wiser and less scrupulous men would have promoted a company, sold, and cleared out again while the demand for shares still ran hot, but Bently and Hansard were, in those early days, more scrupulous than clever. They lived in one bungalow and ate at one table, day in, day out, for three long, sweating, toiling years, until one day a cable arrived for Bently that necessitated his speedy return to England. He scraped together all the ready money to his credit, booked a cheap single ticket in a tramp steamer whose skipper he knew, and shook Hansard by the hand.

"Good-bye, old man," he said.

"Good-bye. If ever you run short while you're at home just cable. I'll find all you want."

"You always were a brick," said Bently, as he stepped into the European carriage on the long white train; "but I don't think I shall have to trouble you— anyhow, I hope not."

The engine shrieked, and the rickety coaches jerked and bumped awkwardly against one another.

"Good-bye."

"So long, old man. Bon voyage. Best of luck." And the train had started suddenly on its way to the coast town, taking with it the only friend Hansard had ever had. He waved his stout malacca until the last white carriage had disappeared round a steep bend in the line, and then, turning on his heel, followed the little group of coolies up the steep path to his lonely bungalow.

There was a soft breeze blowing from the sea, and the gentle flapping of the leaves of the tall rubber trees harmonized with his mournful thoughts.

"It'll be damnable," he muttered between his teeth, "even if he is only away three months."

He strolled slowly away from the shining railroad track and tilted his topi back from his brow. He felt as if something vital had been taken from him; almost as if an amputation had suddenly deprived him of his right arm. Way back from civilization, he must toil and eat and sleep alone for what now seemed an almost interminable gulf of time. No one to talk to, no one to confide in, no one from whom to seek advice.

"It'll be rotten!" he cried aloud as he mounted the verandah steps. "Damn rotten!"

He threw himself into a long cane chair and tried to interest himself in a tattered paper-covered novel until tea-time. Bently's dog—a sharp-faced fox-terrier—came in as he pushed his cup and plate away from him and whined miserably. He got up from the table, threw the dog a lump of sugar on which several ants were crawling, and opened the cupboard door. There were several square bottles on an upper shelf, and he took down one of these already opened. On the floor in the adjoining room he found a bottle of soda-water, and released the glass ball which sealed it with a deft movement of his thumb.

"It's not wise to take spirits before sundown, I know," he muttered. "Bently never would, but today I feel I need something to keep my blessed pecker up."

His hand slipped as he poured out the amber-coloured liquor, and the result was a bigger dose than he had intended; but he did not pour any back into the bottle. He drank the whisky at a gulp, and then, crossing to a small table, started the gramophone. The record was old and cracked, and it clicked terribly at regular intervals.

"It's too awful for words, that damn machine," he shouted. "I wish I'd asked him to order a dozen new records while he was at Singapore. Lord! I can't stand any more of this."

He stopped the shrieking instrument and absent-mindedly poured out another whisky. He shirked his bath that evening and ate scarcely any dinner.

The pig-tailed boy looked at him in surprise.

"Dinner not good?" he asked in Malay.

"Dinner's all right," muttered Hansard.

"*Tuan* ill?" inquired the boy.

Hansard shook his head and swore beneath his heavy moustache.

"Then why not eat the dinner, *tuan*?"

Hansard staggered to his feet, purple in the face.

"Here, clear out of this, you blasted yellow-skinned idol, before I tear your damned tow-shung out by the roots, you—"

The Chinaman turned and fled in terror to the little kitchen at the back of the bungalow, and presently Hansard staggered out on to the dark verandah. He leaned on the stout rail and gazed into the night.

It was still dark, and the stars which dotted the heavens seemed very large and near. Insects hummed everywhere, and the sago-leaf roof rustled gently in a soft sea-breeze. He could just hear the water rippling up on to the sandy beach below. Away far across the valley a watch-fire twinkled, and somewhere a native brass gong was throbbing softly. A stag coughed in the jungle, a pariah dog bayed the moon.

"Lord, but it's damn lonely out here!" said Hansard, feeling in each pocket of his khaki coat for his cigarette-case, and finally tracing it to the table. "To think—that I've—been here—three blessed—years, and only just—found it—out."

He lurched suddenly against the door-post and tried to straighten himself up again.

"Lord," he ejaculated, "I'm as drunk as a pig!"

The Chinese boy, creeping softly on to the verandah with a cup of coffee, laid it gently on the table and hurried fearfully back to his own quarters.

And as the days grew into weeks, and the weeks lengthened into months, Hansard gradually drank himself into a state of drunken stupor. When Bently had been there it had been different; but, then, each had the other's company. The partners had contented themselves with a couple of bottles of lager a day and a small whisky after the sun had set; but Hansard, left to himself, fell the victim to an old craving which he had believed time had quelled. Soon the mandors (overseers) saw it and became lax, the coolies learned of it and grew slack. Weeds shot up unchecked between the rows of rubber trees, water buffalos and deer broke through the wire fences at night, the former trampling the young shoots, the latter gnawing the bark of promising saplings. At last money grew short and bills mounted swiftly up, until one baking tropic day Hansard came suddenly to his senses and saw clearly that through his folly the kabun was almost on its last legs. His friendship for his absent partner turned swiftly to fear, and from fear to sudden hatred. He dared not face Bently. If he could find a purchaser he must sell the estate and fly, change his name, go anywhere rather than meet his former friend again. With an almost superhuman effort he checked to a great extent his consumption of strong liquor, and began to negotiate to the best of his ability for the sale of the Dua-Orang kabun.

II

Arthur Bently, arrived in England, began to find his store of ready money running swiftly out. He had hurried home to attend the funeral of his last remaining relative—an uncle who had passed away in poor circumstances. Many of the necessary expenses had fallen unexpectedly on the young planter's shoulders, but he paid the bills cheerfully, believing that away in the sweltering heat of Borneo he had a friend who would not fail him.

One day, with but a few pounds left in his pocket, he entered the office of an acquaintance and arranged with him to cable to Hansard for money. It was a concise message, and in plain English, before the code book was opened, it read:

"Send me fifty pounds; urgent.—BENTLY."

"Is that all?" asked his friend's clerk, putting down his pen.

"That'll do. I'll call in in a few days for the reply."

"There will be a reply?"

Bently threw back his head and laughed aloud.

"Of course there will!" he cried. "He's my partner out there, y'know."

"I'll send it off immediately, sir. Good morning."

"Good day," shouted Bently gaily, and he ran lightly down the stairs to the busy street.

"What a change from dear old Borneo!" he muttered, as the mighty roar of traffic burst suddenly upon his ears. "Gad! there's not a soul in all this seething crowd of humanity that cares a tinker's curse about me. I shall be glad to be out of it again, by Jove I shall!"

He crossed the road carefully to a comfortable restaurant, where he consumed a hearty and somewhat expensive lunch.

"Dear old Hansard!" he murmured, as he sipped his coffee. "I wonder how he's getting along out there."

He did not think it strange that he had heard nothing from his partner, for he had left him no definite address, and even if he had, both men hated letter-writing. He remembered that he himself had only sent a few cards to the estate from the ports on his way home.

"Ah well! He'll understand," he told himself. A week later he strolled into his friend's office. He had barely a five pound note to his credit now.

"Any reply yet?" he asked off-handedly, in a manner that implied not the least vestige of doubt as to the clerk's answer.

The clerk looked up from some typewritten notes, removed his pen from between his teeth, and shook his head.

"I'm afraid not, sir."

Bently's jaw dropped. "You must be mistaken."

"I'm sure, sir. I see all the cables that reach this office. There has been nothing received here for you."

He tapped a few words on the typewriter, and Bently gazed hard at a dizzy pile of box-files on the opposite wall.

No answer! What could it mean? He put his hand into a trousers pocket and drew out a handful of coins. He must have money in a few days. He slipped the coins back and snatched at a block of scribbling paper on the counter.

"Must have fifty pounds immediately.—BENTLY," he wrote.

"Kindly send that for me as soon as you can. I'm sorry to trouble you again. My partner must be ill."

As he walked slowly down the stairs to the street a thousand fears surged into his brain, but he dismissed them all with a shrug of his broad shoulders. Hansard would not fail him. It was ridiculous. He could hear his farewell words and feel the warm grip of his sunburnt hand. What he had told the clerk must be correct. Hansard was ill, down with fever perhaps. He had been rather a fool to send that second cable. However, he needn't worry himself now. He felt certain the money would be forthcoming almost immediately.

Four days later he received a scribbled note at his hotel. It was from his friend's clerk. He tore the envelope open eagerly and feverishly scanned the contents.

"My God!" he cried, and the whole room seemed to revolve suddenly round him. He clutched at a table for support and stared stupidly at the curt message.

"Dear sir," it read, "cable received to-day; impossible.—HANSARD."

His hand mechanically closed on his few remaining coins, and a cold shiver passed slowly down his spine.

When his hotel bill was settled he had three shillings and a few odd coppers. He took his bag, and, not daring to face the expectant porters, slunk with his eyes on the ground out into the roar and bustle of the great thoroughfare. And all the while, as he strode aimlessly along, something hammered ceaselessly in his whirling brain.

"Hansard has played you false," it said. "He has stolen your share as well as his own."

Barely four shillings between him and starvation! He scarcely dared think of it. Four shillings! It was such a ridiculous sum. He could not remember ever possessing so little. The cabin-trunk of Eastern clothing he had temporarily stored would not fetch very much, he knew. Who on earth wants well-cut suits of "whites" in muddy England?

He stumbled against a loiterer, and looking up as he recovered himself, saw a bright, swinging notice above him, and realized he had wandered into Aldgate, and that night was fast drawing on. The notice was cheering and it read:

"Dutton's Private Hotel. Moderate terms."

Four shillings! He gazed vacantly at a block of unwholesome-looking sweetstuff in an adjacent shop and thought.

Mechanically he felt for his waistcoat pocket. He was dying for a smoke. He drew out a cigarette and tapped it gently on the case. His eye caught the glint of the bright metal. It was silver and fairly heavy. An idea occurred to him. He could raise money on it beyond the slightest shadow of doubt.

He strode boldly to the door of the cheap hotel, pushed it open, heard the sharp clang of an automatic bell, and stumbled noisily up a steep flight of oilcloth-covered stairs. Half an hour later he strolled out whistling gaily. Three shillings bed and breakfast! It was certainly clean and comparatively comfortable, and he could dine where he chose. He had also remembered a small gold watch he possessed. He laughed as he strode into the noisy street.

"I'm getting quite a man of business," he said; and then a memory of the Dua-Orang estate flashed across his brain, and he dug his nails deep into the palms of his hands.

The night drew on as he dived into dirty alleys in search of a quiet house of business where valuables could be exchanged for the much-needed coin of the realm. The thoroughfares grew darker and meaner, huddled, emaciated figures lurked at corners, a woman, her face horribly daubed with paint, spoke to him as he hurried on his way.

"I must get out of this," he muttered, "or I shall lose the little I've got."

Suddenly there came a cry of pain and fear, and a heavy thud on the hard pavement. Bently stopped and listened. The sound seemed to come from a dark passage to his right. He grasped his heavy stick and ran swiftly in the direction of the sound.

Almost beyond the rays of light from a street lamp a well-dressed man lay on the ground with a burly figure kneeling on his chest. A second ragged form was bending over the prostrate man, evidently going carefully through his pockets.

The warm blood surged in Bently's veins. Here was adventure, action—the chance of a fight! He rushed headlong at the foremost hooligan, and tearing him from where he knelt as easily as if he had been a sack of potatoes, threw him heavily into the road. As the second man rose Bently's huge fist met his jaw with a nasty clicking sound. He staggered back into the shadow.

"Come on!" roared the planter excitedly; but there was no response but a scuffling of feet round the corner. Bently found himself handing a purse and a gold watch and chain back to an excited old gentleman, who tried to pat his shoulder and tell him he had saved his life.

"My name's Holloway, sir—Alderman Holloway. Everybody knows me. Only tell me what service I can render you, and you can consider it done."

III

The next morning Bently became Mr. Holloway's private secretary at a small but certain salary. For two long years he endured this uncongenial existence, and every tiresome day he could see the waving lines of Borneo rubber that in reality were his, every night he dreamed of Hansard's treachery. At last, one bright, sunny May morning he awoke to the fact that he was once more a free man, his dead employer having left him the richer for two hundred pounds. He had saved a little money, too, and there was now not the slightest doubt in his mind as to his next move. He gazed tenderly on an old pith topi which graced his chest of drawers.

"I shall go back to Borneo," he said, "and then—" He drew a heavy magazine pistol from its case and held it balanced on the palm of one huge hand.

"Mr. Hansard," he cried, "I hope I shall find you well!"

A fortnight later he boarded the *Prinz Zeiten,* bound for Singapore.

IV

Arthur Bently travelled second class, and by a stroke
of good fortune had the cabin to himself after they
left Genoa. He did not mix with the other passen-
gers, but preserved a sullen silence at meals and had
his deck-chair placed in the most unfrequented spot
he could find. He was aware that this attitude of re-
serve formed an interesting topic of conversation,
but that troubled him not at all.

"Let 'em talk," he muttered to himself one bright
morning after breakfast. He sat in the shadow of the
deck-saloon, and a couple of stout Germans had just
strolled past. He didn't know a single word of their
language but he felt instinctively that they were dis-
cussing him. He felt thankful no well-meaning
busybody had endeavoured to draw him into conversation.

"Oh, damnation!" he grunted, fixing his eyes on
the page he had been reading. "Here's another of
them now!"

He could hear someone approaching from the
other side of the saloon. He just caught a glimpse
out of the corner of one eye of a white skirt flapping
in the breeze. The owner of the skirt stopped suddenly with her back to him and gazed out to sea.

They were steaming through the deep blue waters
of the Indian Ocean, and already the sun was blazing
down upon the canvas awnings. Myriads of flying
fishes sped to port and starboard, skimming grace-
fully over the calm surface of the sea.

Suddenly something borne by the breeze blew
across the deck and caught on his arm, flapping gen-

tly. He started, seized it with one hand, and looked angrily up into the blue eyes of a very beautiful girl.

"Oh, you do look a surly brute!" she laughed, both hands spread out to check a rebellious skirt.

Bently tried to look annoyed, failed, and suddenly found himself laughing back at her.

"Is this your property, may I ask?" he inquired, holding a pink-edged square of cambric between finger and thumb.

"Of course it is," she said.

"It's a very pretty one," he remarked, surveying it closely. He detected a faint suspicion of lavender water; then, thinking a compliment would not prove out of place:

"It's almost as dainty as its mistress," he said, and handed it back to her.

The girl laughed. "That's awfully good—for you," she said, and disappeared round the saloon again. Bently gazed after her with a sigh.

"By Jove! but she's damn nice-looking," he said.

She came back five minutes later dragging a long, cane chair after her. She pushed it next to his, and, taking the novel from his grasp, closed it and pushed it under the cushion of her chair.

"I'm going to make you talk to me," she said. "It's a perfect disgrace for a great strong young man like you to—to behave as you have been doing." There was a pause.

"You aren't really angry with me?" she asked suddenly.

"No." He shook his head slowly. "I don't know, though, whether you ought to talk to me."

"Why?" Her blue eyes opened wide with wonderment.

"Because I'm not fit for any decent girl to associate with."

She sat bolt upright in her chair.

"What do you mean?" she gasped.

"To all intents and purposes—I'm a murderer!"

She sprang to her feet with a startled cry.

"Do you mean you have killed a man?" she cried hoarsely.

"No—not yet," he said calmly.

"You are going to?" She sat back in her chair again and gazed at him in undisguised horror.

"Yes," he said, almost in a whisper, "I hope so."

"I don't think you do—really," she said, and changed the subject.

Dorothy Wentworth and Arthur Bently soon became great friends, and there was still one more subject for general discussion on board the *Prinz Zeiten*. They went on shore together at Colombo, and, seated by her side in the motor he had hired, Bently suddenly became aware that his friendship for her was swiftly turning to something far more serious. As they drove back to the ship through the fragrant Cinnamon Gardens he made a tacit agreement with himself. If Dorothy should promise to be his wife he would endeavour to forget Hansard's treachery and pitch his magazine pistol into the Indian Ocean.

They arrived late one evening in Singapore. As he stood by her side, away from the crowd on deck, he took both her hands and looked down into her eyes.

"This is the last evening we shall spend together," he said. "To-morrow I sail alone for Borneo. It'll be rotten—without you."

She sat down on the end of a long cane chair, and, resting her chin on one hand, gazed over the taffrail at the dark waters. The other hand hung listlessly by her side. Suddenly he stooped slightly and caught it holding it tightly between both his own. She started, and turned her head away from him lest he should notice the warm blood mounting to her cheeks.

"Dorothy,"—his tones were very earnest and very low—"Dorothy, I want you to listen to me. Until I first met you I did not know how good it was to live. The only friend I had ever trusted had betrayed me. I was soured, brooding over the ever-present memory of a great wrong. In my heart there lurked only one dark thought—the primitive instinct of revenge. And then you came—and—somehow I was able to forget for a little while the sole and only reason that was taking me back to the scenes of my early struggles. You showed me that there was something in life better to live for than the pleasure of seeing one's enemy fall. Dorothy, don't you see? Never in my life before have I known a woman who could understand me as you have done."

She uttered a low moan, and the hand within his grasp grew very cold. He slipped one strong arm round her slender waist and drew her closely to him.

"Dorothy," he cried, "I want you—more than anything I have ever desired!"

"Don't!" she moaned. "Please, please don't!"

"I have offended you?"

"No—oh, no. It isn't that. You have been so good to me, so kind; but—I can't explain—you would never understand."

He drew his arm gently away and released her hand.

"I will try," he said simply.

They sat for a while in silence.

"You have not told me yet," he said at last. "Don't be afraid of hurting me. I would rather know it now. Is it—that you do not love me?"

She did not answer.

"Dorothy," he pleaded, "if you care for me even a very little you will be kind to me and let me know the worst. I had thought until this moment that we were made for one another. Our views, our thoughts, our tastes all seemed to lie in the same direction."

She looked up suddenly and their eyes met.

"Arthur," she whispered, "when you first met me—when you first knew that I was travelling alone—did it ever occur to you to ask me the object of my journey?"

He looked down at his finger-nails. "I never worried," he muttered lamely. "I think I rather imagined you were travelling for the sake of your health—to visit a relative perhaps."

"It never entered your head that there is one great reason why young girls leave their homes and put up with the many discomforts a long sea voyage entails? It never occurred to you that I was going out to Borneo to be married?"

His head dropped on to his chest and he groaned aloud. She allowed one hand to rest on his shoulder.

"Arthur, I am dreadfully sorry. You won't believe me when I say so, but I never dreamed that we should come—to this. Arthur, for heaven's sake, don't look like that. What are you thinking! What are you going to do?"

"I don't know—now," he said dully. "My hopes had led me almost to the gates of heaven, and now I seem to have plunged into the nethermost hell. To another man it might not be so terrible a shock, but I—I have not a friend in the whole world—but you."

He rose suddenly to his feet and straightened his shoulders; a look of determination came into his eyes. He held out his hand towards her and looked out to sea. Their hands gripped, and then she held the lapels of his white coat for a moment and looked up into his eyes.

"Arthur," she whispered, "you will always have a friend in me, and perhaps some day we shall see each other again. The world is very small, and Borneo is only a little island. You would not have me break my word to the man who is waiting for me?"

He seized her hand and kissed it feverishly. "You are right," he said hoarsely. "Good-bye." He turned suddenly and strode towards his cabin, his hands deep in the side-pockets of his coat, his head bent low. She called softly after him: "You won't do anything dreadful—now?" But Bently's reply was drowned in the creaking of the deck engines. She sank back into the long cane chair, and burying her head in her hands, sobbed as though her heart would break.

She had promised a man that she would marry him, and nothing could shake her from that resolve; but deep within her lurked something more than regard for the tall ex-planter who had so lately torn himself from her. She could imagine him lying across his narrow bunk gazing at the stars, his strong face lined with silent grief. It seemed so terrible, so hard on both of them. But how much harder would it have been on the lonely, toiling planter who had paid her passage—who was even now counting the hours until she should be by his side—if she had suddenly resolved to marry Bently?

The night air grew chill. She rose, tucked a boat cushion under each arm, and went below.

Back in Api-Api a week later, Bently took up his quarters at the Government Rest-House.

For ten days he lived there, meeting few of the men he had known in the old days. Some had been moved up-country, others had left the Service or were home on leave. Not a word could he learn of his late partner's whereabouts. One day, however, he ran into Mason, who had been D.O. near the Dua-Orang kabun.

"Bently, by all that's holy!" he cried. "We all thought you were dead and buried long ago. Hansard sold the estate soon after you left to a Chinaman, then I lost sight of him until yesterday. D'you know, I rather fancy he must have been in trouble, for he's cut himself off from all his old friends and is managing an estate at Limana, right at the extreme end of the line."

"Is he?" said Bently off-handedly. "I must run down and see him."

He stayed with Mason for nearly a week and then took the train one morning for Limana. He arrived at the next station before the estate at dusk, and, getting out there, strode along the line towards the bungalow

He found the path with the aid of a native guide, and crept stealthily up the slope until the bungalow rose suddenly before him. There was a faint light on the verandah from a swinging oil lamp, and in an inner room the sound of knives and forks suggested a meal. He crawled right up to the verandah and waited, with one hand tightly grasping the deadly weapon in his side-pocket.

A clock was ticking loudly on the verandah, and a small kitten washed itself laboriously, seated at the foot of a long cane chair.

The wind from the sea blew almost chill. Bently shifted his position.

A figure came suddenly on to the verandah. Bently gasped. It was a woman. She crossed to the rail and called:

"Dearest, come and look at the moon reflected in the water; it's so pretty."

Bently's blood ran cold, his hand lost its grip on his pistol, great beads of perspiration exuded from every pore.

The voice was that of Dorothy Wentworth; the man who followed her, and whose arm presently encircled her waist, was his former partner, Hansard.

He stole softly into the shadow of the house. Half-way down the slope of growing rubber he stopped and looked back. Husband and wife were still standing close together, and he knew that she, at least, was radiantly happy.

He drew the dark machine pistol from his pocket and hurled it suddenly into the swamp at the foot of the hill; then he turned, and, his hands deep in his pockets, strode swiftly away into the darkness of the tropic night.

II. THE SWING OF THE PENDULUM

"MERCIFUL HEAVEN! Is it always wrong to hate one's husband?"

Dorothy Hansard, her beautiful young face up-turned in agony towards a deep blue tropic sky, groaned aloud and glanced over her shoulder from the verandah rail to a far corner where, huddled in drunken stupor in a long cane chair, lay George Hansard, the debauched manager of the Limana Estate. Barely a year had elapsed since she had arrived from England to marry the man she loved when he had fallen a victim to the Eastern planter's greatest curse—alcohol! She did not know it had long been a failing of his. She had endeavoured to exert her influence over the weaker vessel, but in vain. From occasional lapses the craving had lured him swiftly on, until it was almost a rare thing to find him sober at all! His assistants worked the estate, sharing the manager's duties for the sake of his beautiful young wife, and as yet the directors at home knew nothing; but she knew, and they knew too, that this state of affairs could not exist for ever. Soon a visiting agent would step from the little white train which ran from the coast town to the Limana terminus, and then—all would be finished. Sometimes, when he paced the bungalow in drunken fury, she almost wished the

end would come. They would be homeless, penni-
less and friendless, she knew full well; but better all
that than this fearful solitude and suspense.

Her life was now a seemingly interminable
nightmare. Sleepless nights, gazing at the big bright
stars which blinked at her from the blackness. Sweltering days when the mosquitos tormented and the
air was hot and heavy. Rarely a soul to talk to, never
a companion in whom to confide her sorrows and
her loneliness. How she longed for the white cliffs
of England, the lights of a busy town, the jingle of
traffic, the whir of a taxi! She had dreamed of the
romantic East as heaven, and found in it a veritable
hell!

Outside, the regular fines of waving rubber-trees;
beyond, the jungle—a vast, mysterious mass of
varying green. Semi-nude coolies toiled in the sun;
solemn, lazy water-buffaloes cropped the luscious
grass in a swampy field. A pigeon, large and copper-
coloured, circled above her; a mongrel cockerel
scratched in the soil in front of the house. A terrier
basked in the sun, endeavouring to conceal a deep
interest in the movements of a brood of young
chicks. She buried her head in her hands and closed
her eyes. Suddenly a memory floated across her
brain of the deck of a huge liner, ploughing its way
swiftly through a calm, blue sea. She could see the
flying-fishes flashing merrily by and feel the soft
breeze on her flushed cheeks. There was a man
seated alone in a cane chair—handsome and young,
yet never mixing with his fellows. She had suddenly
made up her mind to speak to him. She remembered
snatching away the novel he was reading and seating

herself beside him. A warm friendship had sprung up between them—was it only that? Thinking of it now she found herself wondering whether, if she had not been pledged to another, her position would not have been very different now. How sad he had seemed when he came to say "Good-bye"! She started. He had told her he had come East to kill a fellow-man in return for some terrible wrong done to him. She hoped her influence had averted that at least. She wondered if he was still in Borneo, and if he ever had occasion to think of her. Perhaps he had heard of her marriage; perhaps he had tired of the East and had gone home.

She shuddered and sank into the long chair by her side. If she could only have looked ahead, that trip on the German mail-steamer would never have been. She drew herself up and gazed wearily into space; it was no use thinking of that now.

She fell into a doze, and woke a few moments later with a man's name trembling on her lips— "Arthur Bently." Her face grew hot; his memory was dangerously pleasing to her—and her husband snored loudly not a dozen feet away.

She turned over on her side and shaded her eyes with a broad Chinese fan. She began counting the knots in the panels of the wall until at last, weary and heavy-eyed, she fell suddenly into a deep sleep.

The wild galloping of a horse's hoofs, the shrill shouting of Chinese boys and a fearful bellow of mad fury caused her to spring from her chair and run to the side of the verandah. On the ground outside a water-carrier lay doubled up, speechless with agony, while the cook-boy gazed wildly into the distance, one hand to his head, following the retreating figure of a horseman whose mount—a sturdy Borneo pony—plunged wildly from the slope on to the wide stretch of *padi*land, and on, on towards the dark jungle beyond!

"What does it mean?" she cried in Malay.

"The *tuan besar* (manager) is mad," replied the boy. "He has mounted his pony, ridden down the *teucan-ayer*, struck me with his riding whip and has gone—*si-blas-sana* (right over there)."

He pointed a long, grimy finger into the distance.

Dorothy Hansard gazed for a moment at the swaying form fast speeding from her sight, and then, regaining her composure, ordered the cook to carry the groaning water-carrier to the kitchen and send for the first assistant and the black apothecary from the rough hospital on the other side. Then she hurried to her own room and, flinging herself on the bed, sobbed like a child.

"He will be sobered soon and come back," she said, as darkness fell suddenly over the Kabun; but when the sun rose again and the coolies poured from their long, wooden houses to hew and burn and weed, neither the manager nor his pony had returned from that last wild ride.

A week passed by—a week of weary, anxious days—and still no news of the missing manager. Search-parties organized by the assistants had scoured the country for miles and returned each evening without news. The vast jungle had opened its jaws and swallowed both horse and rider.

Alone in her isolated bungalow, Dorothy Hansard lay awake and thought. If she only were certain of his fate. Perhaps even now the birds of prey were pecking at his lifeless form.

"I *must* know!" she cried aloud. "If they cannot tell me I must find out for myself. To-morrow I will start with a mandor and a dozen coolies. Surely the Fates will be kind to me—I have suffered so much already. If I only knew—if I only knew!"

And so in the queer, grey light of early morning Dorothy Hansard rode from her bungalow at Limana at the head of a dusky band of laden coolies to find the man for whom she had crossed nine thousand miles of ocean barely eighteen months before.

Two khaki-clad white men watched the little band from the rubber-grown ridge. As the last dark form vanished beyond the tangled maze of leafy boughs which marked the spot where comparative civilization ended and the wilder country began, the first assistant filled his pipe slowly from a red rubber pouch and turned towards his sunburnt companion.

"Gad, but she's a plucky little woman!"

The other nodded and looked wistfully into space.

"It does seem a damn pity," he muttered at last. "A beautiful woman wasted on a vile beast like that!"

"It's a rotten business altogether," said the first assistant. "There's fever down there in all its fearful forms; there are venomous snakes and filthy, red-haired orangs; there's all the beastly horrors of a vast jungle alive with awful fears—and yet she's bravin' the blessed lot for the sake of a drunken

swine who made her life a perpetual torment!
Women are wonderful creatures."

The younger man grunted and struck savagely in
the air at a huge black flying beetle.

"You'll be manager now, I suppose," he said after
a pause.

"Yes, I suppose so—and you'll have a big lift up
too. I shall have to cable for another junior."

As the two men sat side by side on their ramshackle verandah steps that night, the first assistant
turned to his companion.

"Are you in any hurry for your rise?" he asked.

The other was thinking, and failed for a moment
to understand. "No-o; but why?"

"Because I'd like to wait just a week or two
longer. If he's really dead, they needn't know anything about his failin's, see? He just pegged out,
that's all. Fever, of course. There's any amount die
of that."

"I see," said the second assistant. "The directors
would be kinder to her then; and we—we can easily
wait."

Two brown hands sought each other in the darkness and gripped hard.

Through dense jungle and *padi*-field, through trick-
ling streams and broad rivers, journeyed the little
band. At every village the mandor inquired after the
white *tuan* on the brown pony. Once they learned
that a native had seen a riderless steed, fully
equipped with European harness and saddle, feeding
by the side of a swamp, but, thinking the owner was

near at hand, he had stolen away lest his presence should arouse the white man's ire.

Dorothy Hansard, too weary now to sit her pony, was carried in a *pikul* (hammock) on the shoulders of four stalwart coolies. The native led them to where he had seen the pony, and the marks of its hoofs still visible in the soft soil vouched for the truth of his story. They gave him a dollar and followed the trail for a score of yards, where on the harder ground it ended. They spent a whole day searching in the vicinity, and then, as darkness fell, Dorothy Hansard ordered a fire to be made in a wide clearing and the camp to be pitched for the night.

She woke with a start, and knew by the dullness of the atmosphere that it was somewhere between three and four o'clock in the morning. All around her rough tent sleeping forms lay; some huddled up, some stretched on their backs, their bare arms wide apart, some with their heads resting on wooden Chinese pillars of various designs. It was still dark, although something vaguely indicated that the dawn was not far off.

The camp fire had burned low and cast only a ruddy glow over a very restricted area.

Suddenly her eye caught a shadowy form crawling softly towards her. Was it a wild beast, a huge snake, an ape attracted by the light of the fire? Where was the watchman all this while? It was his duty to keep the watch-fire burning brightly. He must have fallen asleep.

The silent form drew nearer, keeping well beyond the circle of light. She felt for her revolver, her heart throbbing wildly, the perspiration oozing from every pore. The watch-fire, fanned by a sudden morning breeze, burst unexpectedly into flame. The mysterious shadow became solid, uttered a queer, grunting sound and rose before her—black and nude but for a coloured loincloth. He was tall and very broad, and between his teeth glittered the undulating blade of a sharp *kris*.

She uttered a wild cry and pulled the trigger. There was a spurt of flame, a loud report which echoed and re-echoed in the vast forest and a wild, incoherent murmur of human voices, above which rose a fierce yell as of some wild beast mortally wounded in the chase. As the smoke cleared away Dorothy Hansard saw a dark figure writhing in agony, while all around her was chaos.

Weird cries rent the air, weapons clashed and bodies fell crashing to the ground. Ah-Kit, the Chinese mandor, suddenly appeared before her.

"*Mem*, it is finished," he cried in Malay. "We are trapped. There was no riderless pony by the riverside, unless it belonged to the Bajau tribesmen themselves. Come, you must ride your pony again and fly before it is too late."

He caught her up in his powerful arms and ran with her, away from the scene of battle, to where her pony snorted and stamped, tethered to a jack-fruit tree.

He lifted her into the saddle and led the way to where a rough jungle path began.

"There is food in a cloth and a bottle of water," he whispered hoarsely. "The path should lead to Kenapa; there is a *tuan hakim* (magistrate) there. It is about half a day's ride if you go quickly."

He saluted, gave the pony a sudden blow with his cane and disappeared. The pony started swiftly forward, the trees sped past her like weird, ghostly forms in the mists of the dawning day and soon the sounds of the conflict had ceased to ring in her ears. The path grew wider and more clearly defined as the day wore on. Monkeys quarrelled shrilly overhead, a long, orange-coloured snake crossed her track and disappeared into the undergrowth, a hornbill shrieked from somewhere out of sight and a woodpecker tapped in a tall tree.

A native woman carrying a sack of coco-nuts stepped swiftly out of the pony's way and stood still staring after her, wondering who this strange white being might be. Later in the day a Dusun woodcutter saluted and murmured, *"Tabi, mem."*

"I am getting nearer to civilization," she told herself.

Suddenly the jungle ended, and pony and rider emerged on to a broad, open expanse of grass and *padi*-land.

Dorothy Hansard tilted back her broad white topi and mopped the moisture from her sunburnt brow. She heaved a deep sigh of relief and patted the pony's neck.

"You've saved my life, you old dear," she said softly. "Do you hear me? I can promise you plenty of food and rest to-night."

She urged him gently on towards the spot where a broad, *atap* roof just showed on the horizon. Utterly worn out as she was, the sudden change from the dark jungle to the brightness of a glorious tropic afternoon beneath an azure sky put new life and vig-

our into her; the pony, too, seemed to feel the bene-
fit of the change, and quickened its pace.

Suddenly the pony snorted and stood still, nearly
throwing her from the saddle. She stopped and patted its neck. "What's the matter, old boy?" she said.
She looked ahead, shading her eyes with her hand. A
herd of huge water-buffaloes appeared suddenly
from behind a belt of small trees, their broad snouts
uplifted, their tails furiously lashing the air. The colour left her cheeks—of all things in this world she
feared the kerbau most. She had once seen a
wretched Chinaman ripped up by one of those powerful brutes, and she knew well their marked antipa-
thy to white people. Nearer the coast water-buffaloes
are more or less domesticated—dangerous only in
certain seasons—but way back they are a fiercer
breed, as terrible almost as their far Western cous-
ins.

Dorothy Hansard hesitated a second, then wheeled
her pony suddenly round on its hind legs and with a
sharp cut from her cane started it swiftly on a wide
detour to avoid the threatening herd. At breakneck
pace the pony sped over the uneven ground, leaving
a cloud of fine dust, and behind thundered the hoofs
of the dark snorting water-buffaloes, drawing nearer
every moment. Dorothy bent down over the pony's
neck, her hair streaming out behind her, her topi
long flung to the winds. She glanced back. At last
the brutes were being outpaced; soon she would be
safely beyond their reach. Suddenly, as her heart
throbbed wildly in terror, she caught sight of four
more of the beasts right in her path and only a hundred yards ahead. The pony snorted and slackened

its pace. On one side rose a steep bank surmounted by tall trees; on the other the *padi*-fields, in whose swamps the kerbau are more at home than anywhere. Behind them the thundering hoofs of the infuriated herd; ahead the second herd calmly waiting. Suddenly the pony put its foot in a hole, stumbled and threw its rider from the saddle. She closed her eyes—surely this was the end. The trampling of hoofs became like the rumbling of approaching thunder. Her leg was twisted under her, so that she could not rise. The water-buffaloes were upon her.

A loud report, followed by another and yet a third. A slithering of a heavy body into the water; a ghastly squealing and spluttering. She opened her eyes and saw a tall, white-clad form carrying a smoking sporting rifle, a uniformed native by his side.

"Are you badly hurt?" came a cheery, ringing British voice.

"No, thank you, not very much," she tried to murmur, and then fainted suddenly away.

She awoke to find herself comfortably pillowed in a long cane chair on a broad verandah shaded by blue sunblinds. A beautiful Tamil woman, with gold ornaments in her ears, lips, and nose, was bathing her forehead with cool water, and half-sitting on the verandah rail was the broad form of her rescuer.

He was tanned almost a dark brown, and wore a closely trimmed grey moustache. His hair was curly and grey, and his face deeply lined. He was smoking a long cheroot, carefully puffing the long wreaths of blue smoke away from her.

"That's better," he said kindly, as she opened her eyes and looked round.

"How d'you feel now—bit crumpled, eh?"

She tried to speak, but, finding that somehow her voice would not come, nodded instead.

"It was rather a narrow squeak, wasn't it? Now don't you try to answer my foolish questions; just lie still and don't trouble to think. The *ngi* (house-keeper) will get you some soup, and then you must put in as much sleep as you can. You see, I'm D.O. (district officer) and chief medicine man all in one here, and so you must obey my orders implicitly."

A week later Dorothy Hansard sat opposite her host at the evening meal. Insects hummed cease-lessly outside, crickets and lizards called from the wooden walls and the *atap* roof, and a black chow dog was wolfing an enormous meal of meat and rice in a far corner of the room.

"I have inquired in every possible quarter about your husband, Mrs. Hansard," said the magistrate suddenly, "but nobody appears to be able to discover a trace of him. There's only one thing I know out here that can swallow up pony and rider and never leave a trace."

"And that?"

"That is swamp."

She shuddered.

"What an awful end!" she said. "Do you really be-lieve he is dead?"

"What else can one believe?" demanded the D.O., and then: "I'm very sorry, Mrs. Hansard. This deso-late life makes us very brutal at times, but plain facts are plain facts, and there's no getting away from them."

"You are very kind," she said, "and I can readily perceive the force of your argument, but I wish I had only the vaguest proof one way or the other. If I knew he lived it would be my duty to stay here; if I were certain of his death I should go home to England for ever."

The kindly D.O. rose, and, crossing to her side, rested a strong hand on her shoulder. "I wish I had something here to cheer you," he said; "something to take your attention from this tragedy. My gramophone is a vile instrument, and all the records are cracked, and I never had a piano. There are a crowd of grimy novels in that rack over there; they're cockroach bitten and very yellow, but I think some of them are quite readable. Can you amuse yourself with one of them for an hour or so? I am just going across to the village to dig out a native trader I know. He may be able to help us."

He took down a soft, grey felt hat from a nail on the wall and—his malacca under his arm—descended the steep flight of wooden steps to the ground. She heard him bawling loudly in Malay for a lantern and a boy, then crossed to the bookshelf and took out a couple of volumes. In the tiny room, which Dering, her host, styled his "office", a telephone installation had recently been fixed, which connected the bungalow with the nearest railway station fifteen miles away. As Dorothy turned over the soiled pages of the first book listlessly, the bell in the next room suddenly rang. She looked up sharply, and the bell rang again, louder and more persistently. She rose, and, hurrying into the office, lifted the receiver.

"Who is that?" she asked loudly.

"Is that you, Dering?" came a faint voice.

"No. Who is that speaking?"

The voice at the other end was very faint and indistinct.

"Is that you, Dering?" came the voice again.

"No," she shouted. "Mr. Dering is out."

"Oh, will you take a message, please?"

"Yes. What is it?"

"I'm coming across at once, but rang up to tell you. I've found poor old Hansard's horse and saddle."

She gasped, reeled back and dropped the receiver. It struck against the wall, and part of it fell off and rolled along the ground, but she did not stoop to recover it.

Then Hansard was dead; his pony and saddle had been recovered. She sank into the nearest cane chair, and resting her chin in her hands, gazed out into the blackness of the tropic night. So this was the end of it all! She didn't know whether she felt really sorry; had he lived he could have been only a helpless burden upon humanity—drink-sodden, vicious, useless!

She could not mourn for him as she had known him since her marriage, but her heart went out to the handsome, nobler creature she had known in those far-off early days in England—the boy who had gone East to work for her. She felt that *he* had died almost a year ago, after the first glamour of their wedded life had faded away.

Suddenly she sprang to her feet and hurried to the telephone. She stooped and searched for the portion of the receiver that had fallen. It was just a black ring that had come unscrewed. She readjusted it and listened. She could hear nothing but the singing of the wires. She had not asked who her informant was.

"Are you there? Are you there? Hullo!"

Still no answer; perhaps he was already hurrying on his way. She found herself wondering who he was.

She picked up her novel and read for more than a couple of hours. Suddenly there came the clattering of a horse's hoofs on the hard pathway below. The bungalow was mounted very high above the ground on stout poles, and all was darkness outside.

"Hullo, there!" came a clear, ringing voice. "Boy! *Mari sini* (come here). Take my horse, *lakas* (quickly)."

Dorothy Hansard started. She seemed to have heard that voice somewhere before. She shrugged her shoulders and laughed derisively her nerves were unstrung, she told herself; she was full of foolish imaginings. She heard the boy leading the beast to the rear of the bungalow, and then the sound of footsteps on the stairs; the stranger was coming up on to the verandah. Her host was out still, so she must remain there and receive his visitor. The lamp which swung from the ceiling had burnt rather low, and the top of the stairs was almost in shadow. A tall, broad, well-proportioned man, dressed in a well-cut suit of whites and carrying a broad topi under his arm, stepped suddenly on to the verandah and stood before her. She rose to her feet and advanced a step.

"Good evening, madam. Is Mr. Dering about?"

"Good evening. Mr. Dering is out. Won't you sit down? I'll call the boy to wait on you and attend to the lamp."

He sat down a few yards from her. She tapped a small Eastern gong, and the cook-boy hurried in.

"Fetch the *tuan* drinks," she said in Malay. "Whisky—soda," added the stranger. "And then turn up the lamp if there's still oil in it."

"There is plenty oil, *mem*," replied the boy, and he stood on tip-toe in front of the visitor and turned up the wick. As he stepped from the verandah the eyes of the man and woman met.

"Dorothy!"

"Arthur!"

The man rose, and, turning half away from her, bit his thumb-nail and groaned.

"Isn't this just cursed Fate all over!" he cried bitterly.

She left her chair, and, crossing the verandah, placed a slender hand on his broad shoulder.

"Why, what do you mean? Aren't you pleased to see me after all this time? Have you forgotten what friends we were on the *Prinz Zeiten*?"

"Heavens, no! Forgotten? Lord! I've tried hard enough, God knows!"

"What do you mean?"

He turned fiercely round upon her, and then, meeting her eyes, mechanically felt for her hands and held them tightly. They sat down facing one another on opposite sides of the same broad cane chair.

"Dorothy," he said suddenly, "I came here to-night to tell Dering of your husband's fate."

"I know," she whispered. "I answered the telephone. I did not know it was you."

"His pony was found straying by one of my men, and they brought it down to my house."

"How did you know it was his?"

"Listen. Now he is dead I can tell you. Years ago Hansard and I shared a small estate down Dua-Orang way. The sudden death of a poor relative—my sole remaining relation—called me home at short notice. In my absence Hansard denied me money that was mine. He sold my share of the Kabun as well as his own and cleared. I was stranded in England with never a friend to turn to for assistance. One evening, absolutely on my uppers, I saved a queer old gentleman from some roughs. He made me his private secretary, and when he died two years later he left me a little money. I started off for Borneo, as you know, and on the way met you. We became great friends. You forgot to tell me you were engaged to be married, so I, when at last I saw your ring, went away to seek my enemy, never dreaming that you were his affianced wife. I crept to his bungalow one dark night and waited. I had a heavy pistol in one pocket, and my finger was on the trigger. I was waiting for him—Hansard—the man who had left me to starve, who had robbed me. I did not know then that he had robbed me *of you* as well."

She gasped and tried to draw her hands from his grasp.

"Let me finish my story. When I saw you together on the verandah I knew the worst. Fate was against me, my luck was out. I threw my pistol away, and for your sake forgave him. I And then fortune favoured me in every way. I dealt in copra and rubber and coco-nuts. I dabbled in tobacco. I risked everything because I didn't care, and somehow I always came out on top. I knew your husband's pony by the saddle and harness and by the beast itself for, believe me, they were all mine."

She suddenly withdrew her hands and buried her face in them. Her shoulders heaved ominously. Arthur Bently was speaking again in his old soft, natural tones, just as she remembered him on board the German liner.

"Poor little woman!" he whispered.

"They tell me he beat you, that he was never sober, that he made life hell for you."

She uncovered her eyes and turned her tear-stained face to his. "Don't," she whispered, "don't say that, Arthur. Remember he is dead."

Arthur Bently drew her close to him until she could feel his hot breath on her cheek.

"I want you to forget he ever lived," he said, and kissed her unresisting lips.

III. *SAMSU*

ALONG THE ROUGH JUNGLE PATH sped the sturdy Borneo pony at breakneck speed, its nostrils dilated, its brown neck flecked with foam. On its back, reeling from side to side, but retaining his saddle by the aid of that mysterious providence which seems to exert a special care over drunken men, sat George Hansard, manager of the Limana Kabun. His shirt was open wide at the neck, he was hatless, and his riding breeches gaped open below each knee. The wild rush through the air, rather than sobering him, seemed to have had an almost opposite effect, for every moment he grew more reckless and the flush on his cheeks became more vivid.

"Faster, faster, faster!" he cried, thrashing the pony with his riding-whip and digging his knees into the poor beast's sides. The pony stumbled and then recovered itself. The path became more and more uneven, until at last there seemed scarcely a track at all. A huge branch just passed over Hansard's hair, brambles lacerated his face; he bent lower over the pony's neck, but never attempted to check the awful speed. He was mad—mad with the effects of months of imbibing strong liquor—and his fuddled brain longed for something refreshing, cooling. He had hoped to find it in the atmosphere, but it was mid-afternoon, and the air was heavy and very still. A flying beetle struck his face and held on with its sharp claws. He dashed it away with his left hand and cursed it as it fell, buzzing loudly, into the matted undergrowth. Suddenly he rose in the stirrups and shouted wildly, incoherently:

"On, on, on! Get a move on, you brute beast! Hi, hi, hi! Faster, faster, faster! *Pergi jaland lakas!*"

The pace became terrific. Twice he was almost hurled from the saddle, but somehow, when great overhanging branches had been left yards behind, he was still clinging limpetlike to his mount. A native woman in a highly-coloured sarong and a belt of silver rings dropped the basket of fruit she was carrying and fled into the jungle shrieking aloud in terror. A pariah dog ran on to the path and snarled at him, backing behind a coco-palm as he drew nearer. A small sloth ran along a bough above, a giant ape paused on its way from tree to tree to hurl a branch in his direction, and a huge iguana darted clumsily over the ground to the safety of a tall palm.

Hansard's brain had ceased in its working. He only saw a queer green blur, a vivid and ever-moving curtain on either side of him. He had forgotten his comfortable bungalow on the hilltop, his beautiful, patient young wife, his two loyal assistants, the trusting band of directors at home, far away in remote old London.

The landscape suddenly changed, the trees became farther and farther apart, the atmosphere seemed fresher and purer. He inhaled a deep breath as the pony dashed through a dozen yards of tall rank grass, plunged knee-deep into water, snorted, stopped suddenly short, and hurled its rider into the turbid waters of a broad winding river.

Hansard hit the surface of the water with a loud splash, sank, and then rose, snorting and spluttering, till his great brown arms mechanically executed a clumsy breast-stroke and his heavily-booted legs buffeted the stream in a desperate endeavour to keep his body afloat. The pony stood where he had left it a moment before, then, snorting suddenly in terror, plunged from the river bank into the jungle again and was gone from his sight. He could hear it galloping wildly into the distance as he splashed and spluttered in the muddy stream, and then his eye caught something which made the blood run cold in his veins and his damp hair rise almost on end. An ungainly, lumbering form, not unlike a fallen tree trunk, slid suddenly from the opposite bank into the water, and came slowly but very surely in his direction. Merciful heaven! A crocodile! Its awful snout was but a dozen yards from him. Still half-drunk and heavily weighed down, he could make little progress to escape from it, and he was unarmed!

Desperately he rolled over on to his back and splashed the water wildly, like an awkward child learning to swim. The brute veered slightly from its course, but did not stop. A queer snuffling sound to his right caused him to turn his head suddenly. He screamed aloud and splashed with awful vigour. A second snout had appeared above the surface of the river barely three yards away, and a third was visible close behind it. He cried aloud again, and a mist rose before his bloodshot eyes. So this was the end of it all—this was Bently's revenge! Fate was on the side of his old trusting partner whom he had robbed years ago, and she was playing her cards only too well. The pony, the very harness, he now remembered, were Bently's. He could see him as he left the Dua-Orang Kabun on his way home to bury his sole remaining relative. He remembered how he had promised him money, and when the cable came from England refused it, and left his partner to starve, friendless and alone, in a crowded city. And now, at last, Bently's turn had come.

He could splash no longer. He dared not open his eyes, but he felt—he knew—that the dreaded snouts were just closing in upon him. *Sudah habis*—it was finished!

Suddenly there came a wild shout in a hoarse native voice, and a wave of water washed over his head. He struggled desperately and opened his eyes. The crocodiles had retreated a little and a large dugout canoe, manned by a tall, swarthy native, was speeding in his direction.

"Lakas!" he cried hoarsely. "Quickly, I drown!"

A pair of cunning eyes surveyed him as the hands with the paddle ceased to move to and fro.

"What will the white *tuan* give me if I save him?"

The man was a Dusun, and he spoke in a mixture of Malay and his own dialect.

"Anything—everything I have!"

"What is anything—everything! Is it money, precious stones, gold and silver?"

"God in heaven, be quick, before these brutes seize me! Are you human? I shall be torn to pieces."

"There is a risk that in saving you I shall overturn my boat and perish with you," replied the Dusun coldly. "It is not for nothing I hazard this."

"I am manager at Limana—I have much money there."

"Limana is a long way off, and I dare not venture where the police are found, for they have long put a price on my head. Is there nothing in your pocket?"

"In my pocket? I have a gold watch and a heavy silver cigarette-case."

The canoe came closer, a black hand caught his arm, and, deftly maintaining the balance of the frail craft, the Dusun drew Hansard up beside him and began beating the water with his stout paddle in the direction of the three hideous snouts.

There was a pile of merchandise at one end of the boat, coloured sarongs, bright shawls and cheap jewellery intended to adorn the ears, noses, or lips of dark native women. Hansard, somewhat sobered after his immersion, muttered a few words of thanks in Malay and almost mechanically drew off his wet coat and threw it into the bottom of the canoe at the trader's feet.

"The watch and case are in there," he said. "It's a big price for the little you did; but I'm not a dirty Dusun, so I keep my word."

The dark trader sat down opposite him, and, shipping his paddle, clutched eagerly at the dripping garment. He weighed each article in his hand before thrusting it into his sarong.

"So it was but a little thing I did for you, oh, white *tuan*?" he inquired insolently, thrusting the paddle deep into the stream. "Is your life so valueless? You

did not think so a moment ago, when the crocodiles'
ugly snouts were seeking their meal."

Hansard rid himself of the remainder of his clothing, and, selecting a couple of sarongs and a conical
hat of native woven straw, lay back on the pile of
cloths and regarded the spare form of his rescuer.

The Dusun trader was taller than most of his kind,
and very thin. He wore a straw head-dress, black
with age, a coloured sarong, and a short coat of
black velvet fastened with three huge silver
brooches of native manufacture. A thin, drooping
moustache ornamented his upper lip and his chin
displayed a faint suggestion of beard. His eyes were
small, and sparkled like live coals; his face was
lined and very pock-marked.

"Where are we going?" demanded Hansard suddenly, as he idly watched the dark waters swirling
along. The Dusun eyed him cunningly. "*Sa-na* (over
there)," he replied coolly; and, resting his paddle on
his knees, commenced to fill a filthy, charred bamboo pipe with tobacco which resembled coco-nut fi-
bre.

Hansard flushed furiously. The native's insolence
annoyed him, and he was not at that moment in a
mood to brook an insult.

"You blasted idiot!" he shouted. "Where is this
blessed '*sana*'? Where does the river lead to? Come,
you *kiti*, none of your dirty games, or I'll throw you
over for the crocs to make *makan* of. Where are we
going?"

The trader slid his oar deliberately back into the
water and commenced to paddle vigorously onward,
an evil expression adorning his swarthy face.

"I have a house," he said softly, "back where no white man's foot has yet trod. My boat is fast taking you there."

His eyes seemed to bulge suddenly from their sockets.

"You remember I told you when you cried to me for help that I dare not risk a meeting with the white *mata-mata* (police). All white men are alike my enemies—all are allied against me. I—who once in fair fight took a white head with one blow of my *parang* (sword). Do you think, then, *tuan*, that I can dare to let you escape, and perhaps betray me? I have no desire to hang in the sun for the birds to peck at, or to risk the swift bullets from a white man's *snapang* (rifle). Henceforward, *tuan*, you are in my power—I, who dragged you from the crocodiles' mouths. You must come with me to my lonely house under the palm trees, far from the places white men inhabit. Food you shall have in plenty and freedom to do as you please; for if you wander too far the jungle will swallow you, and there is much forest between my home and the great Limana Kabun."

Hansard crimsoned beneath his tan, clenched his huge fists, and sat suddenly upright.

"Here, you black scarecrow," he roared, "turn that damn boat round *baniak lakas* (very quickly)!"

The trader laughed aloud and plied his paddle with still greater vigour.

With a mighty oath Hansard flung himself upon him, his great hands seeking the Dusun's dark neck. The canoe rocked violently and shipped some water, the trader uttered a queer hissing sound between his two perfect rows of gleaming teeth, and the planter staggered back, feeling for the place in his chest where a gleaming native *kris* had made a slight incision. The Dusun slid the weapon calmly back beneath his sarong and eyed his prisoner keenly.

"Remember one thing always!" he snarled. "I have taken many heads in war, and my aim is very true."

The paddle dipped once more into the dark waters of the stream, and the little boat sped swiftly between thickly wooded banks. Monkeys shrieked in the trees, and a long green snake stole softly up the bark of a coconut palm. Sometimes, as the river narrowed, the interwoven boughs of trees formed dark tunnels through which they sped into the tropic sunlight on the other side. As the hidden chorus of humming insects heralded the approach of darkness the trader lit a battered hurricane lamp, doubtless stolen from a far-off plantation, and hung it at the bow. Night fell suddenly, the jungle stirred and woke, and Hansard shifted his legs into a more comfortable position and shuddered.

"Lord!" he cried, "it's damn desolate back here! If we run into a snag we're done. For God's sake go carefully, or we'll feed the crocodiles yet!"

"I know the river as I know myself," replied his companion calmly.

There was a pause, and then Hansard said, "I'm getting deuced thirsty. Haven't you anything aboard worth drinking?"

He could just see the outline of the Dusun's dark form still plying the paddle as if his arms were incapable of succumbing to fatigue. In the nickering

light from the lantern he resembled some weird
fiend from the lower regions.

"There is plenty of water," he replied shortly.

Hansard shrugged his shoulders impatiently and
swore. The trader drew a flask from somewhere beneath him and handed it to his companion. The
planter wiped the top carefully with his hand, took a
long pull, spluttered and vomited into the stream.
"Trying to poison me, you devil?" he asked, still
spitting violently over the side.

The Dusun chuckled. "That is *samsu*, the native
spirit," he said. "You will like it soon; I have nothing else but that in my house, except milk and water,
and those white men do not drink."

Hansard groaned, turned over on his side, yawned
once or twice, stretched himself, and fell suddenly
asleep.

When he woke the canoe was being thrust through
tall-standing rushes by the river's bank. It was still
dark, but somewhere beyond the reeds a second lantern was approaching them, apparently borne by
someone who was cautiously threading a way down
a poorly defined, winding pathway.

Suddenly a shrill voice echoed in the stillness, and
was answered by the trader, who had now gained the
bank and was dragging the canoe alongside for Hansard to step out. The Dusun guided him a few yards
and then hung his lantern on a bough above them, as
a native woman, lamp in hand, came into the circle
of light. She was small and well-formed, her slender
form enveloped in a long green sarong stretching
from her breasts to her bare feet.

"I have brought a white man," said the trader. "He had fallen in the river and the crocodiles were seeking him." Then, turning to Hansard, "This is Marani, my daughter. Come, we must eat. The hours have been long, and my arms are tired with the toil of the day."

Five minutes' walk led them to a small clearing, in the centre of which, approached by a tall bamboo ladder, a small, squat native hut rose on long poles, for all the world like a very long-legged spider. Hansard, still half-dazed and very tired, followed his companions up the tall ladder and crawled after them through the tiny opening which served for a door. A smoking oil-lamp hung from the roof, throwing its faint rays on to the bare-boarded floor, the sago leaf walls, and the insect-infested *atap* roof above. Hansard shuddered. To live his days, and, worse still, his nights, in this reeking atmosphere! No mosquito curtains, nor even a decent pipe of tobacco to smoke. A mosquito's shrill note suddenly broke upon his ear, and he hit wildly behind his head in the darkness. A large fat spider crossed the floor leisurely, disappearing swiftly when the girl stretched out her hand towards it.

As Hansard lay half asleep on a native mat that night he overheard a conversation between Marani and Dahamin, her father. The trader was crouching by the door of his hut, a shawl round his dark shoulders, and his daughter squatted on the ground by his side chewing betel-nut and spitting into the darkness.

"My father, I am glad you have returned," she said softly, "for I believe that you have an enemy, and that he is ever watching for you."

The Dusun uttered a hoarse exclamation.

"It was three nights ago, and I sat where you are now sitting, softly beating a gong and wondering when my father's canoe would come safely back over the miles of water, when suddenly I thought I heard the faint sound of crackling twigs over there beneath the big coco-palm. At first I believed it to be but an ape crossing the clearing, and then my heart became still. A dark form stood for a moment in the light of the moon, and, as my hair rose on end and my blood ran cold in my veins, it was gone again, and all was silent."

Dahamin turned on his daughter and gripped her arms so tightly that she cried aloud.

"Marani, are you sure of this?"

She nodded.

"It was a man, you tell me?"

"Yah, bapa, a man like yourself, but taller."

"Taller than I?"

She nodded again and fidgeted with the silver bangles on her wrist. The trader's face was hideously distorted as the lamp flickered and burned suddenly brightly.

"Was he—a white man?"

The girl shook her head. "His face was very dark," she whispered, "and his dress was as all Dusuns wear."

"I thought that nobody knew my hiding-place," he muttered presently, and then, with a sudden bellow of rage, plunged his hand beneath his sarong and leaped to his feet, the sharp *kris* gleaming in the lamp-light. Hansard heard the ladder creak as the Dusun hastened to the ground, and five minutes later saw the trader's form darken the entrance once more.

"You were right, my child," he said hoarsely, "there is someone lurking in the shadows, watching, ever watching. If, as you say, he is not white, it is a thief who covets my riches and my merchandise. I will seek a dog in the nearest village; meantime, look well, Marani, that you always keep your sharp *kris* in readiness beneath your sarong."

A stag coughed in the darkness, and somewhere an owl hooted dolefully. Hansard dropped soundly asleep, and did not wake again until the sun was high in the heavens.

The days passed by, and still the planter lived with the Dusun trader and his daughter in the primitive dwelling beneath the palms. Sometimes he would be left to himself for hours, and then the solitude became awful and the craving for strong liquor almost unbearable. Exiled from all he had ever cared for, from his own kind, from the little comforts he had been always accustomed to, Hansard learned something of what his wife's existence must have been during those awful months when he had saturated himself ceaselessly in spirits. Seated on the bare-boarded floor, his feet on the upper rungs of the rickety ladder, he would smoke fibrous tobacco in a rough bamboo pipe and picture his old home at Limana in the rings of blue smoke curling skywards.

If he could only steal the canoe one night while the trader and his daughter slept and paddle swiftly back to comparative civilization—to even the first magistracy! Lord, how he craved for the sight of a white face, the grip of a British hand! He must return to his wife, give up strong liquor, take his turn once more in the development of the estate, and make amends for all those awful months of drunken idleness. But as the sun grew hot all higher thoughts were dispelled, and he dreamed only of spirits. What would he not give for a glass of whisky and soda— to watch the myriad bubbles travelling to the surface of the amber-coloured liquid, to feel its pleasant sting in his parched throat? And every evening the cunning trader would produce a bottle of the terrible *samsu* and snatch it suddenly away before Hansard, who had now acquired a taste for it, could drink more than was good for him. The Dusun knew full well that one day, when it might be necessary to silence his prisoner for a while, he had only to leave that earthenware jar of fermented liquor near at hand.

One late afternoon, while Hansard paced the clearing impatiently, a shrill whistle came suddenly from somewhere in the jungle to his right. He turned sharply and picked up a pole near at hand.

"Who the devil's that!" he muttered; and then, pursing up his lips, whistled shrilly and waited. There was a pause, and then the whistle came again, this time from somewhere close at hand. Hansard passed a weary hand over his brow. "I could have sworn—by Jove! the 'Cock of the North'—almost the identical bars!"

A dark figure stood in the clearing—dark-skinned and in native costume; but the voice was scarcely that of a Dusun.

"Well, I'm damned!"

Hansard started back. "Who, in God's name, are you?" he cried. "And what the devil are you doing in that unearthly garb in this God-forsaken hole?"

The newcomer advanced towards him and extended a big brown hand. Hansard gripped it hard.

"Well!"

"Well!"

They looked into each other's eyes and laughed heartily.

"What are you doing here?"

"Well, what are you?"

They both laughed again. The newcomer grasped Hansard's arm and led him swiftly from the clearing into the jungle beyond.

Once secure from possible interruption, the stranger turned to his companion and said, "My name's Mellor. I'm doing a little detective work up here in the wilds. It's a sort of hobby of mine, and the bosses at Api-Api have commissioned me to track down a blood-thirsty blighter of the name of Dahamin. He's badly wanted for one or two crimes, and is as slippery as a blessed eel. Know him?"

"I should rather say I do. I'm in the brute's clutches myself."

Mellor whistled, and Hansard told him his whole story from the very commencement of his troubles.

"Then you're Hansard!" cried the other as he finished. "You're the planter who disappeared so mysteriously from the Limana Kabun. Jove! but I'm in luck to-day. Think what kudos I shall get from un-earthing you! Hullo! Somebody in the clearing. Meet you here to-morrow. So long."

Their hands gripped, and he crept silently away through the trees. Hansard strolled leisurely back to the hut, and as he emerged from the forest came face to face with Marani, Dahamin's beautiful daughter. She was standing very erect, a basket of fruit balanced on her head, regarding him curiously.

"My father is still away?" she asked in Malay. Hansard nodded, threw the pole he was carrying high in the air, and caught it as it fell.

"As I came through the jungle I thought I saw a man stealing through the trees at a place where the leaves are thick. You have seen nobody, *tuan*?"

Hansard fixed his gaze on a small fly which hovered in the air in front of him and shook his head.

"There has been nobody here," he said. "I am glad you have come back, it's been damnably lonely."

The girl climbed up the steps and pushed her basket into the tiny doorway. She looked down at him over her shoulder.

"What would you do if a thief stole into the clearing and found you here alone?"

Hansard regarded her queerly.

"I suppose I should try to kill him," he said.

"But you have no weapon, *tuan*."

Hansard started, and remembered the conversation he had overheard on his first night in the native hut.

"I should be powerless!" he cried eagerly. "The man would surely carry a *kris*."

The girl looked him straight in the eyes and drew a shining weapon half out from the folds of her sarong.

"The white *tuan* would like to have this very much," she said; and, laughing musically, disappeared through the doorway into the hut.

Hansard passed his hand through his matted hair and over his bearded chin. "I wonder what the little devil's getting at," he said, and began to fill his bamboo pipe from a little leathern bag she had given him soon after his arrival there.

On the following day he again met Mellor in the jungle near the clearing. "Mellor," he said, "I must get away from here, and it's up to you to help me— you know the country and I don't. I want to get back to my wife and the Limana Kabun. I want to see a barber and get a decent trim up. I want to taste decent food and sleep in a decent bed. Lord, you don't know what I've suffered these last few weeks! It's been hell—absolute hell!"

Mellor smiled grimly and puffed at his blackened briar.

"I've tasted some of the delights of the lower regions, too," he said, "and now the atmosphere's getting a bit too hot even for me. I'm being watched, I believe, by someone or other, and I must clear back for reinforcements before I can capture my man. Tonight I help myself to our friend's canoe and start on the return journey. If you wish to come with me you must be at the riverside over there about an hour after sundown. If you are not there I shall presume you are too closely guarded, and shall start back alone, in which case you must wait until I return with the police. You understand?"

Hansard nodded. "I understand," he repeated. "I shall be there, never fear."

Mellor stretched out a brown hand. "Till an hour after sundown," he said, "good-bye."

"Good-bye."

Suddenly Hansard called softly after him: "Mellor, I say!"

"Hello!"

"I'm absolutely without a weapon of any kind. Can you spare me a pistol?"

The detective shook his head.

"I have only one for myself, and I may want it before long. Still, you must have something. Here, take this! It's a pretty useful article, you'll find." He drew from under his clothes a long horn-handled hunting-knife, and Hansard grasped it eagerly.

"Thanks, old chap," he said. "I feel a different man now."

He closed it and thrust it out of sight, then turned sharply and strolled towards the river's bank to the spot Mellor had indicated. He noted every bend in the rough path which led from the hut. There must be no obstacle in his way, he told himself. He swallowed a lump in his throat as a vision of his beautiful young wife rose before him. He could see her tear-stained face, her arms outstretched to enfold him. He could feel her in his grasp, her hot breath fanning his cheeks, her warm caresses. Soon he would be by her side again, a reformed man.

Somewhere back there in the jungle Mellor, who had opened the road for his escape, was waiting for the darkness to fall. The girl Marani was busily grinding *padi* at the back of the house, singing monotonously as she worked. Dahamin was selling his wares in the adjacent Dusun villages; he had told him his day's programme before he left. Hansard felt certain he would not venture back until he and Mellor were well on their way towards civilization. Everything seemed to be working in his favour today. He tilted back his conical straw hat and wiped the beads of perspiration from his forehead with the sleeve of the tattered khaki coat he still wore.

"Lord! I'm feeling damn thirsty," he said to himself. "I'd give anything for a glass of good beer."

He sat down on a fallen tree trunk and regarded the cool waters idly.

"That river seems to be somehow woven into my life," he muttered. "It was into that river Bently's pony threw me; it was there I nearly lost my life when Dahamin pulled me out and drove off those blasted crocodiles; it will be on the waters of that river that I shall pass to-night from servitude to freedom, from degrading poverty to comparative luxury." He surveyed the bare calf of his leg and sighed. "It's a wonder I've not been carried off by fever long ago; I'm one mass of mosquito bites and jungle sores. How long the time seems! In another hour at the most it should be dark."

He surveyed the surrounding landscape critically. The dark waters of the reed-grown river had long ceased to appeal to him, the varied green of the jungle bored him horribly, the shrill cries from the monkey colonies in the tree-tops irritated him.

"I want a clean bed, a white suit, and a good meal!" he cried to the jungle. "Please heaven, I'll have them soon!"

He looked suddenly up and caught a glimpse of something round bobbing up and down in the stream quite close to the river's bank. He started to his feet and advanced a couple of paces towards it. Holding on to the overhanging branch of a tall tree, he leaned forward until his fingers just touched the floating object. It disappeared beneath the surface, and then bobbed up again, a foot farther away, in a most aggravating manner. One thing, however, Hansard had seen—it was an earthenware bottle, its seal unbroken! *Samsu*, that intoxicating liquor, the taste for which time and necessity had taught him to acquire! He sat down again and looked towards the jungle.

"Mustn't touch it," he muttered. "Must keep a cool head for to-night."

His eyes wandered from tree to tree, from the leafy boughs to the reeds rustling in an afternoon breeze. He felt that he must allow himself just one glance at that queer round bottle. How far had it travelled, he wondered, since he turned his head? He looked. The earthenware receptacle lay on the mud not a couple of yards away, the water lapping gently round it. He looked nervously over his shoulder, like a naughty child fearful of being caught at some forbidden act, seized the bottle in both hands, and ran with it into the forest. With the hunting-knife Mellor had given him he dislodged the round, flat cork and peered inside. Then he held the bottle to his nose and took a long sniff. Lord, how thirsty he was! Surely it would do no harm to have one little sip—

just a taste to relieve the dryness of his parched palate? He put the bottle to his lips, and the promised sip became a prolonged gulp.

The *samsu* that fatal river had borne to him was old and very strong. He reeled, sat heavily down, and drank again. His eyes grew misty, the jungle seemed to revolve suddenly round him. "I'm drunk," he ejaculated thickly, "beastly drunk!" and then fell fast asleep where he lay, the precious bottle slipping from his grasp and pouring its contents over his sarong, his khaki sleeves, and on the leaves of the weeds at his side for the flies to revel in.

At one hour after sunset Mellor stepped softly into the canoe and looked around for his companion. Hush! What was that? A man snoring in the undergrowth? He listened again and laughed. A stag was coughing in the jungle near at hand; no doubt that was the sound he had heard. Evidently Hansard was too closely watched to attempt an escape that night.

He thrust his paddle into the river and the frail barque sped swiftly down the stream, while Hansard slept his only chance away.

IV

OFF THE BEATEN TRACK

FROM THE LEAFY SHELTER of the jungle, Dahamin, the Dusun trader, watched his enemy speeding down the turbid river in his—Dahamin's—canoe. The night was very dark, and he could not recognize the thief, but he felt instinctively that it must be someone with quicker brains than Hansard; besides, Marani would be watching their white prisoner too closely. Who could it be? The man whom he had seen spying on him just after Marani had whispered to him her suspicions? A thought struck him; perhaps the spy was hired by his enemies, the white officers of police, to reveal to them his hiding-place; perhaps he was even now hastening for reinforcements! The trader gritted his teeth fiercely. The spy must be overtaken at all costs!

He ran wildly down the jungle path and up the rickety ladder. Just inside the doorway of the hut Marani, his daughter, was busily weaving a basket, choosing her coloured strips of *rotan* by the dim light of the smoking oil-lamp which swung from the low ceiling.

"Apah mahu?" (what is the matter?), she asked, glancing up from her work as he threw himself panting at her feet.

"Where is the white *tuan* I left in your care?"

She shrugged her pretty, dark shoulders and laughed. The trader raised a threatening hand.

"Come, this is no laughing matter. Tell me, where is he?"

"He is sleeping in the jungle, drunk with *samsu*, snoring like the pig that he is!"

"Drunk with *samsu*? Where did he find the liquor?" He seized her arm and shook her roughly, so that the half-finished basket slipped from her grasp and rolled away across the floor. "You have not shown him my hidden storehouse *sana*? (over there?) You have not told him where I keep my *samsu*?"

"I cannot tell you where he found the liquor," she moaned in Malay. "I only know that he is drunk and snores. Listen!"

In the silence which followed the raising of her finger, the loud, regular breathing of a heavy sleeper became audible from somewhere in the jungle near the hut.

"It is well—he sleeps," grunted the trader, feeling in his belt for his bamboo pipe. He filled the bowl deliberately, and then turned on his daughter in sudden fury. "Why did I trust in you, you hoonoon, blind fool that you are! Where is my boat? Gone! Where is my secret hiding-place? Gone! No longer is it a secret; it will soon be known to all the world. The white *mata-mata* (policemen) will come swiftly here in their *engine-kapal* (steam-launch), and you will yet see your father strung up between earth and sky for the birds of the air to feast upon. I tell you that, while you waste your time with foolish baskets, a thief has stolen our canoe and gone—gone towards the coast."

The girl ceased sobbing and looked up at him, trembling with fear and emotion.

"The boat is—gone?"

"Yes, gone! Have I not already told you? The boat that has served me so well, that has carried my merchandise so long."

Marani picked up a stray end of rotan and twisted it into a loose knot.

"My father is very strong, can he not follow the man and recover the canoe? Has my father forgotten the old canoe where the *samsu* is hidden?"

Dahamin leaped to the ground with a sudden effort and stood at the foot of the bamboo ladder gazing up at her.

"Quick! A lantern and a *parang* (sword)," he cried. "There is no time to lose. Ere the day dawns, Marani, your father will have taken another head."

"And then," added the girl thoughtfully, "it will be time to seek a new hiding-place."

She handed him a sharp, curved weapon in a wooden sheath, ornamented with tufts of human hair, and turned to seek the lantern.

Hansard woke from his drunken sleep and sat suddenly up.

"Daylight!" he cried. "Merciful heaven! it can't be day yet." Then the awful truth dawned upon him, and he buried his head in his hands. He had found the intoxicating Chinese drink—the powerful *samsu*—and had drunk his senses and his only chance of escape away. Mellor had waited for him in vain and was now doubtless well on his way to reveal Dahamin's hiding-place to the nearest district officer. Still rubbing his eyes, he rose slowly to his feet and marked time for a moment with each leg.

He hurried towards the river-bank and looked everywhere for the canoe, but it was gone. At the most important point in his whole career he could not quell his craving for liquor, and so the opportunity of escape had come—and gone, perhaps, for ever. The trader, missing his canoe, was certain to suspect that his movements were being closely watched, and would seek a better hiding-place, where Hansard, helpless in the wilds and dependent upon him for food, must perforce follow him.

"When Mellor returns with his men," he told himself, "I shall be gone. Poor little Dorothy! I shall never see her again nor the bungalow down at Limana. I suppose Dane is manager now, and lives where I spent so many happy years."

A shadow crossed his brain.

"I wonder where Dorothy has gone? Perhaps she has believed me dead and gone home to England; she was never very happy out here. Borneo's the very devil for women!"

He emerged from the jungle and crossed the clearing towards the foot of the frail ladder.

"Marani!" he called loudly.

"Yah, *tuan*." A pretty black head was thrust through the aperture in the wall.

"Is there any *makan* (meal) this morning, for I'm fearfully hungry?"

"The white *tuan* was very drunk last night," she said reproachfully, "or he would have seen a thief who stole my father's boat."

Hansard whistled and stood looking up at her, one foot on the bottom rung of the ladder.

"So the boat has gone, has it?"

She nodded.

"And my father has gone quickly after the thief— in an old canoe he has not used for many years."

Hansard looked hard at one bare foot. A vision of a swarthy form tirelessly manipulating a paddle rose suddenly before him, and he shuddered. He knew Mellor had a revolver, but he also knew that the trader was cunning in the extreme and took no risks.

"How far was the stranger ahead?" he demanded suddenly.

"Not thirty minutes, *tuan*."

Hansard's blood ran cold.

"May the old canoe sink!" he muttered, and climbed up the stairs to take the two green bananas Marani held out to him.

As he reached out for the fruit he lost his balance for a moment and clutched at her wrist to save himself from falling. He steadied himself, but somehow retained his hold on her arm.

"*Baniak chantek* (very beautiful)," he ejaculated suddenly, looking full into her eyes.

The girl looked down and tried to withdraw her hand, but Hansard held it tightly.

"If your father does not come back, what will you do?" he whispered.

Marani shrugged her shoulders and laughed, revealing two perfect rows of white teeth.

"He will return," she said. "He is very strong and brave. There is no man can row so fast as my father. He will kill the other man and return with two boats before evening. He is a clever man, my father. Will the *tuan* let me go? My wrist is hurt."

Her free hand slipped suddenly beneath her sarong. Hansard realized the significance of her sudden movement just in time, and before she could raise her hidden weapon to strike had caught both her wrists and dragged her with him to the ground, struggling and biting like a wild creature.

He wrenched the sharp, undulating blade from her grasp, and thrust it into his belt near where the hunting-knife Mellor had given him lay hidden. Then he caught the dark form in his arms and drew her to him.

"You are too beautiful to be his daughter," he said hoarsely, and rained hot kisses on her neck and cheeks.

She did not attempt to free herself now, but simply gazed at him, her eyes open wide with amazement. When at last he released her from his close embrace she turned and ran up the ladder into the house without a word.

Hansard sat suddenly down, and, drawing her *kris* from his belt, began testing its sharpness on the woodwork of the ladder.

"She's damn pretty," he muttered half to himself, "and the chances are I shall never see my wife again."

He hacked at the bamboo for a moment in silence.

"Anyhow, a man must live, and there aren't many luxuries out here in these Godforsaken wilds."

Half an hour later Marani came swiftly down the ladder and sat down by his side. He slipped one arm gently round her waist, and a black hand rested confidingly on his broad shoulder. Hansard laughed till the jungle re-echoed the sounds of his mirth!

"To think of it!" he cried. "And an hour ago I was afraid of you, you wild little cat!"

"Perhaps even a wild cat is less to be feared when deprived of its claws," she whispered softly.

The two slender black arms were round his neck now. He bent down and kissed her fiercely twice. Suddenly her eye fell upon something fine and yellow encircling his neck. She touched it, and then seized and pulled it hard. It was a thin, gold chain, and she drew from under his coat a large gold locket, heart-shaped.

"What is that?" she asked, turning it over in her hand.

"What's what?" His thoughts had been far away.

"This pretty thing." She held it close to his face.

With a fierce oath he rose to his feet, flinging her roughly from him. He crimsoned beneath his tan. It seemed a sacrilege that black hands should touch this keepsake—a wedding-present from Dorothy. He had sworn never to part with it. Inside there was a faded photograph of herself as he had first known her, in those dear, far-off days in England—before he had thought of the East, and rubber, and all the vile temptations of the Tropics. "Never part with this," she had said, "until you part with me for ever!" It had sounded foolish, melodramatic, at the time, but now those far-off words seemed to have a prophetic ring. It seemed almost as if she might have anticipated all this. He pushed the locket back under his coat and pulled the collar up well over the thin gold chain.

Marani looked sullenly up at him from where he had thrown her. Her pretty lips pouted and her bosom heaved tumultuously.

"It is pretty, and I want it," she said.

Hansard deliberately buttoned his tattered khaki coat and swore fiercely in the Dusun dialect.

"When you can take it from me, you little *hoonoon*, you can have it," he shouted scornfully, and rattling his *kris* against the hunting-knife at his waist he strode swiftly towards the river-bank to watch for Dahamin's return.

As soon, as he was out of sight, Marani hastened through the jungle to the secret store where her father kept the spirit that had proved Hansard's undoing.

"When I can take it from him it will be mine," she said, and hid an earthenware bottle beneath the folds of her brightly coloured sarong.

Darkness had fallen not half an hour before over jungle and swamp, plantation, and *padi*-field, and over the little court-house at Kenapa. Myriads of insects hummed in the cool evening air, the shrill, piercing note of the mosquito, the deep droning of some flying beetle. Down in the swamplands giant frogs croaked noisily, and out in the darkness a pariah dog bayed the moon until his hoarse-voiced complaining grew monotonous.

Dorothy Hansard lay back in her long cane chair, the novel open in her lap unread. She was thinking—thinking deeply. It was now many weeks since her husband had ridden madly into the jungle never to return. Of course, he was dead. It would be ludicrous to think otherwise. His pony had been found straying, fully equipped with the harness it had worn when he went. Hansard was dead, and Arthur Bently—handsome and prosperous—had asked her to marry him, and she had consented. She had never really forgotten Bently, she told herself. Through all those months of nightmare, when Hansard had raved and cursed under the influence of liquor, she had always had before her a vision of that German mail-steamer and a handsome man who had looked so sad when he saw the engagement ring on her finger.

How small the world really was! She had treasured this little romance for her very own, and never breathed one word of it to her friends or even to her husband. It had been like a beautiful, sunny landscape, painted by a great artist, to whom death had come before he could put the finishing touches to his canvas. She knew now that Arthur Bently was the only man she could ever love. What had made her marry Hansard she did not know—perhaps it was just that strange affection, that cheap imitation of higher feeling, that brings about the union of a farm labourer in a tiny village with his next-door neighbour. She had known Hansard when they were children together, and because of that fact had consented when, hot-blooded and impetuous, he had begged her to confer on him the greatest happiness his life could ever have.

It all seemed so strange and so wonderful that Arthur Bently, who had stolen her affections from her husband, should be the very man Hansard had wronged and betrayed, and left to starve in England years before. It looked as if Fate had deliberately thrust her finger into the crucible of life when her particular romance was being concocted by the hidden powers who control this great orb and its myriads of toiling atoms.

A terrible thought floated suddenly across her mind. Suppose Hansard was not really dead—that when she was married to Bently and they were living happily together Hansard should suddenly walk in upon them! Bigamy! It was an ugly word, and the world looked upon it as a terrible crime. And then what would happen, if after all those years, Arthur Bently should come face to face with George Hansard, the man who had so cruelly wronged him, whose life he had determined to take. She shuddered and closed her eyes as if to shut out the picture her vivid imagination had suddenly conjured up. Dare she marry Arthur and risk this remote possibility?

A heavy step on the long flight of stairs which led from the ground below to the broad verandah, a cheery greeting, two great muscular arms thrown suddenly round her and eager, warm lips seeking her own. She did not resist his embraces—he seemed so strong, so magnificent. By his side she would risk anything.

And so the vision of the missing planter vanished from her mind, and the living reality of Arthur Bently occupied her mind in its place. She pillowed her fair head on his broad shoulder and murmured inarticulately. The language of love is not conveyed by mere words; it is a sort of vague Esperanto handed down from time immemorial—common to all races and kinds.

A Chinaman with a swinging lantern hurried past the courthouse to his home somewhere beyond that shadowy belt of trees to the left. A terrier dog ran out from under the house, barked at him, and then returned, growling fiercely. An owl hooted mournfully, and a cloud passed over the moon.

Dorothy Hansard shivered involuntarily, and Bently's arm held her still more closely to him.

"You have not changed your mind?" he asked suddenly.

She shook her head and pressed her lips against his cheek.

"You will marry me soon?"

"When you wish, dearest."

Arthur Bently rose suddenly, lifting her gently to her feet.

"Let us lean on the verandah rail," he said. "I want to look out on the night. D'you know, I love the darkness out here even more than the glorious sunlight. It shuts out everything and everybody—but you. Hark!"

In the little office behind them the telephone bell rang suddenly. Dorothy started, her heart beating wildly. It was on that same telephone she had heard of the discovery of her husband's pony—from Bently's own lips. Perhaps—

She listened intently.

Dering, her host, was speaking.

"Hullo! Who is that? Oh, Fox! How are you, reverend signor? Quite well, eh? What's that? Going to pay me a friendly call to-morrow? Good; I shall be delighted. Not seen your face for months. Be here to midday, *makan*, can you? Good. Bye-bye!"

The bell rang again as Dering replaced the receiver.

The two by the verandah rail were silent for a while, and then, as the moon emerged from behind the cloud-bank and flooded the verandah with its pale rays, Arthur Bently caught her hands in his and looked into her eyes.

"To-morrow, then?" he whispered.

"Very well, Arthur," she replied softly; "to-morrow."

Yes, Fate certainly seemed to juggle strangely with their futures, for, oblivious of all else in the intoxication of their great happiness, they did not guess that Mellor was fast speeding in a stolen canoe to break the news that Hansard was alive and well.

A white-clad Chinese boy coughed warningly to announce his entry with a lamp. Dorothy Hansard took up the novel she had discarded, and Bently stooped to shade a match with his hand and light a fat, gold-tipped cigarette.

Alexander Mellor pushed out into midstream from the reed-grown bank.

"It's damnably dark," he muttered, "and there must be a deuce of a lot of snags about. Still, I must take my chance as I've done all along up to now. I wonder what's kept Hansard, and whether the same cause that is detaining him is spying also on me?"

He dipped the paddle into the water and, with one last fleeting look at the spot where he had arranged to meet the planter, started down the stream at an ever-increasing speed. Mellor had rowed in his College eight years ago, and had worked almost every kind of water craft in existence; but he did not know the river as Dahamin, the Dusun trader, knew it. His ignorance did not make him afraid; his nerves were not strained to breaking-point as an average man's would have been in such a case. He had a wonderful confidence in his own good fortune and a strange knack of just scraping through. "If a cat has nine lives," they used to say at Api-Api, "then Mellor has at least eight."

For an hour he paddled vigorously between thickly wooded banks, finding his way through the intense darkness more by instinct than anything else. Wild creatures started back from the stream as he flashed by, uttering strange growling and gruntings as though objecting to this human trespassing on the hours that were their own.

"Infested with crocs, I bet," he muttered as he plied the paddle lustily. "If I do overturn—*sudah habis*—it's all up with me."

It was lonely work out there where human foot had scarcely trod, and, brave man that he was, he found himself forced first to whistle a gay music-hall ditty he remembered hearing when last in town, and then to sing aloud a boisterous chorus. When the last echoes of his song had died away the silence became awful, as if the whole world had suddenly ceased action. A wild cat howled miserably near at hand, and something large near the left bank was snuffling and splashing heavily in the water. He did not see what it was, but he could make a pretty shrewd guess.

"Rhino," he said aloud. "Lucky I didn't run into him in mid-stream."

He paddled on for an hour, and then a sudden thought struck him. He was hastening on his way to fame; every stroke drew him nearer to it. He could reveal the secret hiding-place of Dahamin, the dark-skinned murderer whom all others had sought in vain. For that alone promotion would be certain. At the first magistracy he would announce his discovery and send a messenger for the men necessary to effect the capture. He could almost feel himself on board the Government steam-launch on his way back to slip the handcuffs on Dahamin's wrists. Then there was the solution of the mystery that had baffled everybody—the sudden disappearance of George Hansard. He pictured Mrs. Hansard's joy at learning the glad news of the husband she had supposed dead. Mellor had seen her once at a dance at Sandakan, and remembered telling a friend she was a "deuced pretty little woman". He raised his paddle from the water and let the canoe travel some distance by itself. Gad! how he had suffered! And yet now, when he was well on his way to civilization, it seemed worth it—every bit. What a time he would have with the boys in Api-Api! Champagne?—he had almost forgotten the taste of it.

"Poor old Hansard!" he said suddenly aloud. "He'll have to wait a little while longer, I'm afraid, for his decent clothes and barber and bed."

The moon sailed suddenly from behind a cloud, and something made Mellor glance back over his shoulder. He started, and the beads of perspiration stood out on his forehead. Behind him, perhaps a hundred and fifty yards distant, another canoe was coming along the stream at a fearful pace, propelled by arms that seemed to work with almost diabolical fury. Who could it be? Not Hansard, surely? None but a native could attain that awful speed. Mellor dipped his paddle into the water and urged his canoe along as fast as his tired arms knew how, at intervals looking back over his shoulder to see what progress his pursuer had made.

Suddenly the whole truth dawned upon him. Dahamin—the Dusun trader, who knew every inch of the river! The man in the other canoe must be he! Dahamin—the head-hunter, the murderer! Dahamin—dreaded by all who knew his record!

Mellor's blood ran cold, and he paused for a second to loosen the revolver in his belt. This sudden development was distinctly annoying to him. He had wanted to take the trader alive, not have to drag his filthy corpse to Api-Api! That seemed the only alternative, for, if Dahamin escaped him now, it would be for ever. He must lure the native as far as he could, and then, on rounding a bend, slip into the reeds by the bank, and shoot him as he sped by in pursuit. The plan sounded well in theory, but after the next tunnel of interwoven boughs the jungle grew sparse, and open *padi*-fields replaced the forest-covered banks of the upper reaches of the river— and Dahamin was fast gaining on his enemy.

Mellor drew his revolver from his belt, and, holding it between his knees, thrust the paddle once more into the stream. His blood tingled in his veins, his nostrils dilated. Here at last was excitement—a fight to the death, and may the best man win. Dahamin, fast closing on his antagonist, stood up in his frail craft and cried aloud—excitedly, inarticulately. He, too, throbbed with the promise of battle, and this was his war-cry, his signal of warning to his foe. In the boat before him lay a sharp Dusun *parang*, unsheathed, and a long, queer-looking tube with a spear-head at one end. By its side rested a bamboo cylinder, about a foot in length and three inches in diameter. He sat down in the canoe again and sent it hissing through the dark waters.

"The Good Spirits are with the dog," he muttered, "or the river would have had him long ago. But he will need all their help to save him shortly, for I, Dahamin, have spoken."

And Mellor, bending low, swung his paddle mechanically from side to side, his left arm every now and again giving a sharp twinge which heralded an attack of cramp. Ahead there was at last a wooded bank; if he could only reach that and ambush his pursuer!

"I've nothing much to fear," he muttered at last. "He has but a sword, while I have a six-chambered revolver waiting for the beggar."

He was not aware of a certain terrible engine of destruction rolling to and fro in the bottom of the canoe at the Dusun trader's feet.

Dahamin rose suddenly, when barely twenty yards separated the two boats, and placing the long bamboo tube to his lips puffed once! Something brushed past Mellor's shoulder and fell into the water just ahead. "A fallen twig," he murmured, and then glanced back over his shoulder. Dahamin was paddling furiously once more. Mellor turned and made one last desperate effort to gain the shelter of the trees, and Dahamin rose in his canoe once more and, retaining his balance perfectly, puffed something through the tube again. It just missed Mellor as he swayed to the motion of the paddle and fell at his feet in the bottom of the canoe. It was a long, white piece of thin wood, perhaps seven inches in length, with something like a cork at one end and a black fluid staining the other. Mellor's blood ran cold, and the perspiration started from every pore.

"My God! he cried hoarsely to the night. "The *sumpitan*! If he hits me I'm done!"

A third poisoned dart, with power to kill in ten short seconds, hissed past him. He ducked low over the canoe, felt for his revolver, turned and fired wildly in the direction of his pursuer.

Dahamin laughed aloud. "Huh!" he cried. "A white *tuan*! There will be another white head for the police to avenge!"

He dropped his tube back into the boat and raised his paddle.

Something flashed in the darkness again; there was a loud report, and the trader felt as though a red-hot iron had suddenly been forced through his left arm. He screamed wild Dusun curses to the woods, and, dropping his paddle, found the tube and puffed a tiny dart once more at the man ahead. In the light of the moon Mellor saw the deadly arrow flash, and dodged aside to avoid it. It missed him by a hair's breadth, but the canoe, thrust suddenly from its course, encountered a half-submerged tree trunk. The bottom was ripped away, and Mellor, uttering a wild cry, dropped his weapon and slid with a splash into the stream.

Dahamin's war-note re-echoed once more in the stillness, and, manipulating his canoe dexterously by means of his one sound arm, the Dusun trader drew near to the spot where the detective, unarmed, still struggled in the weed-grown waters. Even as the trader approached his enemy, as his right hand dropped the paddle and reached for his sharp-edged *parang*, a terrible cry of agony broke upon the stillness of the tropic night—and Dahamin understood. He saw the upturned face of Mellor, and its expression was as that of a soul in torment. He knew instinctively that the dark waters of the river were being rapidly stained with human blood.

"The brutes shall not rob me of my revenge!" he hissed, and, seizing the hair of his antagonist before the white face finally disappeared beneath the surface, he whirled his sharp *parang* aloft, and a moment later threw a severed human head to join his weapons in the bottom of the boat.

V. THE DAUGHTER OF DAHAMIN

THE DAWN ROSE IN THE EAST, and the first white light which heralded the coming of the sun shone upon the winding river, the dense jungle which merged on to its banks—and Dahamin, the Dusun trader. He had drawn his canoe up on to the bank a mile farther down the stream than where his enemy had perished, and Mellor's head, wrapped in palm leaves bound together with tough, thin rushes, lay with his sword and *sumpitan* in the bottom of the boat.

He ran his frail craft out into the water and swore fiercely as he remembered the fate of his newer boat that Mellor, in his efforts to avoid his deadly darts, had wrecked upon a snag the night before. He paddled gently along still down the river towards a spot where he fancied bananas might be growing. The sun came up as he glided softly over the still waters, and the colourless dome above changed suddenly to an ever-deepening blue. A huge brown hawk hovered in the heavens, and a flock of rhino birds flashed like a streak of silver light across the stream a hundred yards ahead. In the bright light of early morning the jungle trees were very pleasing to the eye, and the cool river rippled gently to a slight breeze.

Dahamin laughed aloud for the very joy of living, and kicked the hideous relic at his feet.

A black form suddenly appeared on the right bank of the river, and a Dusun woman bent down over the stream to fill a gourd with water.

"Tabi!" shouted the trader, waving his paddle in the air.

The girl started and looked up in surprise.

"Tabi!" she replied, and, placing the gourd on the bank at her feet, stood with her hands on her hips surveying the newcomer with interest.

"*Deri mana?* (whence come you?)" she said at last.

Dahamin pointed with his paddle back over his shoulder.

"*Deri si-blas-sana* (from right over there)," he replied. He paddled close into the bank, and, holding on to a low branch which jutted out over the water, looked calmly up at her.

"Any news to tell me?" he inquired, plucking a strand of grass and chewing it.

"*Tida-tahu* (I don't know)," she replied, looking thoughtful. "They have ceased to look for the drunken white *tuan* whose pony ran away with him many weeks ago."

Dahamin laughed, and cracked his fingers thoughtfully.

"They seek him no longer? Well, is that all?"

"Let me think a little while. Ah! I remember. There is a white man in native clothes and with blackened face seeking the mad trader Dahamin—he who once murdered a white man."

The Dusun started and then laughed.

"They will never find him," he said. "He is far too clever for that."

"You have seen him?"

"Never. He has gone *sa-na*—far away over the hills where the white men dare not venture.

"I have heard, also, from my sister, who lives with a white *tuan* at Kanapa, that the Mem Hansard will soon marry another white *tuan*, for all the world knows the *Tuan* Hansard is long dead."

The girl turned away, and the trader called softly after her: "Hi! *sini* (here), I am hungry. Can you find me some *pesangs* (bananas)?"

The girl whispered *"Berhinti!"* (stop) and disappeared into the bushes. Five minutes later she returned through the leafy screen, a bunch of small green bananas in her hand.

"Here!" she cried gaily, and threw them to the trader.

"Prima-kasih," he replied, as his brown hand arrested their flight. He tore them greedily apart, and the speed with which he consumed them testified to the keenness of his appetite. He cast the skins over the side of his canoe into the water and idly watched the half-submerged mass of green float slowly out of sight; then, catching hold of the overhanging bough once more, and securing his boat to it by means of a length of coarse rope, he commenced to fill and light his charred bamboo pipe.

"The pretty maid has time to talk to me?" he inquired, as a small cloud of dark smoke rose skywards.

"When the sun is low in the sky," she said, splashing in the water with her toes, "it is not wise to waste the moments, for when the noonday sun beats down it is not easy to save them again."

Dahamin gazed up at her with admiration. Hardened rogue and homicide that he was, he still retained his native taste for loveliness in woman. To his eyes the girl was beautiful. He admired the roundness of her arms, the fullness of her bosom, the coils of thick black hair that shone in the early morning light like a raven's wing. It was dangerous, he knew full well, for him to venture too near the realms of law and order; but somehow he wished to talk to her—her charm seemed magnetic.

"And so the *Mem* Hansard has found another husband?"

"Yah, I have already told you."

"And the other *tuan* dwells at Kanapa?"

"I did not say so."

"No, but you told me you had news of all this from your sister, who is a white man's *ngi* there."

"You are clever enough to be a *mata-mata* (policeman). What is your name? You are a stranger, it seems, in these parts, or you would surely have known all I have told you."

Dahamin nodded, and smoked for a moment in silence. The girl climbed down from the bank and stepped lightly into the canoe. She sat down opposite to him, and pushed the palm leaf bundle aside to make more room. Her sharp eye suddenly fell on the *sumpitan*, the tube which puffed the deadly arrows that bring death in an instant.

"So," she whispered, "the stranger has hunted through the night. What does he find to kill on the river banks? Is it monkeys he seeks?"

The trader apparently did not hear this last question, for he only replied to part of the first.

"Yes, pretty one, I am a stranger to these parts," he said, looking far away to where the river turned suddenly from its straight course and vanished in a network of overhanging branches. "I am a poor trader, and returning from my toil of yesterday. The darkness caught me, and I had perforce to spend the night upon the river's bank."

"A trader?" Her eyes opened wide in wonderment. "But where are your wares?"

The Dusun started, knocked his pipe noisily on the side of the boat, and recovered himself.

"Yesterday I had a good day of business, my merchandise was all bought from me before the setting of the sun; and so, light of heart, I did not notice the approach of night."

"Then you have money instead of goods—*baniak ringit* (plenty of dollars)?"

The trader nodded. "Under my sarong there is a leathern purse, and such as I have is there."

The dark eyes sparkled. "Oh! you will show them to me?"

"Why do you wish so much to see them? Dahamin was not prepared for so much questioning.

"You think that I would steal them." The thick lips pouted and the trader bent forward to kiss them. The black girl stepped quickly away from him, seized the branch to which the canoe was moored, swung neatly on to the bank, and pushed the trader smartly before he could regain his balance. With an oath he slipped suddenly sideways and fell with a loud splash into the river.

The girl stepped swiftly into the boat and picked up the parcel tied together with palm leaves and reeds. She laughed as the Dusun splashed in the water, endeavouring to obtain a hold on the steeper part of the bank towards which he had drifted.

"You lied to me!" she cried. "Your money is not in your belt. It is here, in this bundle." She tore at the thongs with her slim fingers, and then bent her face towards it and bit at them.

"Put it down!" cried Dahamin. "It is *honto* (haunted)!"

The girl laughed, and began to unwind the wrappings.

Dahamin struggled furiously to climb the bank and prevent her seeing what the leaves contained. He dug his nails into the soft soil, almost reached the top, then slipped and fell back into the shallow water again.

Suddenly the leaves fell away and the grisly relic lay revealed.

The girl uttered a wild scream which echoed and re-echoed in the stillness of the tropic morning, then dropped the severed head and fled swiftly away, her hands to her ears, shrieking, until the monkey colonies in the trees above her joined in a chattering chorus.

The trophy rolled awkwardly down the slope, wedged in the thin mud between a tree trunk and the bank, and lay gazing up at the trader, as he scrambled at last to the summit and hastened to recover it.

The terrible screams, the utter absence of all other sound, the look in those eyes which stared so strangely up at him awed even the hardened Dahamin. Cursing furiously, he leaped back into the boat, threw the head into the bottom, and paddled with the energy of one possessed back up the river again, striving to shut out from his ears the ringing of those terrible screams.

"I should never have stayed to speak with her," he muttered, when more than a mile of water lay between him and the scene of the discovery. "Women are never to be trusted. And now she will tell the people of her village, and they will say, 'Yah, this is indeed the work of Dahamin!' The peaceful Dusuns will then send word to Kenapa, and they will call out the black police and their cursed white officers. The great *engine-kapal* will thrust its snout into the upper reaches of the river, and they will think to smell out where the head-hunter lies. I must move my house—very quickly; and just now I am poor, and I have lost my best boat."

He paddled in silence for a long while, never lifting his eyes from the stream. At last a notion seemed to strike him, and he sat up suddenly and rested the paddle on his knees.

"Can I trust the *Tuan* Hansard?" he muttered. "If I can trust him I may yet be rich. I remember on that day when I pulled him from the river—yes, from the very jaws of the crocodiles—he kept his word to me and gave me the price I asked. Yah, that indeed was so! He has told me also that he—a white man— always kept his word. When the liquor is not in him he is just."

As the old familiar bends of the stream drew nearer he laughed aloud and splashed in the water with his paddle.

"I shall go to him and say, 'Dahamin is merciful, and he trusts in you. Listen! In my journeyings to and fro with my merchandise I have heard that the *Mem* Hansard will soon marry another *tuan*, and believes that you are dead. There is but one man who can bring you swiftly back to her—that is I, Dahamin, the trader, the head-hunter! Tahu? You have told me you had much money at your kabun in Limana. See, now, how I shall trust in you. On a night, soon, I shall take you, at the risk of my head, to the river near Kenapa, where your wife now dwells. On the following night you shall return to me alone, and bring with you one thousand dollars. A small thing, *tuan*, to you, but a fortune to such as I.' Thus shall I speak to him, and he will gladly agree. Perhaps, even, the price is too little? I must think well over this. After that, Marani and I will fly still farther away from the dwellings of the white men, and trade and trade and trade until the thousand dollars will have become thousands and tens of thousands. Then will I dress her as a princess, and sell her, perhaps, to some chief of a great village."

He laughed again and spat over the side.

"The white *tuan* will be glad," he said at last, "when he hears how small a time his wife has wept for him."

Hansard sat by the water's edge, near the spot where the canoe had been wont to be, and thought. His pipe had gone out long ago, but he still held it firmly between his teeth, and sometimes sucked thoughtfully at the mouthpiece.

It was nearing midday, and the sun was beating down upon the parched earth. Even in the shade of the tree where he lay the atmosphere was almost unbearable. All round seemed desolate, deserted, and to-day the voice of Marani was not heard singing, as was her custom when working in the hut or round the clearing. Marani—yes, she was young and pretty as black women go. Not a patch on Dorothy, his wife, of course; but still, he must put Dorothy out of his mind, for he could never see her again. He had led her a dog's life during those last few drunken months before he rode madly away into the jungle, passing like a flash from her life. It was the golden locket Marani had discovered round his sunburnt neck that had reminded him of her. He had told Marani she could have it when she could get it, which he swore to himself would, of course, never be. He would hide it while he slept in case her native cunning should prompt her to come in search of it, and he would wear it always by day. He buried his head in his hands and his shoulders shook. He had never loved his wife so much as he did at that lonely moment way back where white man's foot had scarcely ever trod.

If he could only, by some means or other, get back to civilization, turn over a new leaf, refuse all strong liquor, put himself in her hands, and try to make up for all the hell he had caused her to endure—if only Fate would smile on him for once—by heaven! he would make any sacrifice only to be near her voice, to hold her hands. He wondered if she had forgotten him, if, even now, convinced of his death, she was fast nearing England on some great ocean liner homeward-bound.

England, and bright lights, smart shops, and well-cut clothes! He surveyed his reflection in the water and turned away in sudden fury. He was bearded, and almost black with the sun. He wore a tattered, weather-stained khaki coat over a coloured sarong reaching down to his knees. On his head was a battered straw hat, conical in shape, woven in many-coloured rotan by a native woman. His sandals were of grass, such as the coolies wear—those toiling, sweating beasts of burden little higher in the scale of life than the water-buffaloes that wallow in the mire of the *padi*-lands. His hand, wandering over the various glaring defects in his barbaric costume, travelled mechanically to his leathern waist-belt, and thence to two shining weapons thrust between the buckle and his body. The one was a keen-bladed native *kris*—he had wrenched that from Marani—the other was the sharp hunting-knife Mellor had given him that afternoon before he (Hansard) had found the deadly *samsu* and drunk away his only chance of escape. Liquor had been his ruin all along, he remembered. It had made him betray his old partner, Arthur Bently, years ago and rob him of his rightful share in the Dua-Orang Rubber Estate; it had thrust insurmountable barriers between his wife and himself; it had caused his final wild ride on his pony's back into the unknown. He had been a fool to himself, and now he was paying for it to the very last cent, reaping in the same manner as he had sown.

He drew out the long hunting-knife and examined it minutely; he tried it on the ground and on the trunk of an adjacent tree. It was very sharp, and might serve him a good turn yet. He was still strong in muscle. Armed as he was, he was surely a match for the wiry Dusun trader—his gaoler? He must encounter him before Marani could speak to him, and force him to turn his canoe and take him back the way he had brought him months before. Supposing he did not return? Supposing Mcllor had shot him as he sped after him in wild pursuit? Then he must stay until the police launch came at Mellor's bidding to find him. If the months went by and Mellor forgot his promise, there was always Marani.

He rose from where he had been sitting and went stealthily down the bank for half a mile or more, determined to intercept Dahamin on his return and force him to take him back. Fully armed for the first time since he left Limana, he felt a man again—his confidence in himself had partly returned. Anyhow, he felt equal to arranging matters with the trader. There was no intoxicating liquor to tempt him now; nothing should turn him from his path. Under pretence of friendship he would call Dahamin shorewards. The trader did not know he was armed and would be sure to come to him, even if only to discover why he had ventured so far from the clearing. He would lure him from his boat, and then—there was the hunting-knife. It should not take long to persuade Dahamin. He pictured the swarthy Dusun suddenly paddling down the stream back to civilization—to white suits and white faces—while he (Hansard) sat, knife in hand, opposite him, urging him to exert himself still further that the weary miles might not seem too long. The shoe would be on the other foot this time, he promised himself. If he had trouble with the trader he would take him to the nearest magistracy, and there was a heavy price on his head. If he behaved himself, Hansard resolved that he would let him go and return unmolested to his hut, for the sake of that dark-eyed little witch, Marani.

Hansard sat down in the bushes and waited. Perhaps he would not come at all; perhaps even now the handcuffs chafed the trader's wrists. Hansard had already great faith in Mellor's prowess. He began to calculate how long it would take him to bring the little government launch round from Api-Api to where he now lay sheltered from the sweltering heat.

"Lord, I *am* getting thirsty!" he groaned. "How much longer is the blighter going to keep me here? Not a drop of anything drinkable in sight! If I try river water I shall only be courting typhoid."

He shifted his position and filled the bowl of his home-made bamboo pipe with fibrous tobacco given him by Dahamin. He drew a box of Chinese matches from the torn pocket of his dilapidated jacket and puffed.

"Gad! what a thing a pipe is!" he murmured, resting his face in his hands. "I don't know what we men would do without this little pet vice of ours. Hello!"

He crouched down in the undergrowth and peered through the boughs towards the bend in the stream. A bird had flown suddenly from a tree, complaining shrilly of some serious disturbance, and somehow Hansard felt instinctively her perturbation was due to the approach of the canoe whose owner he was awaiting. He listened intently. From somewhere still a long way off came a faint, measured splash-splash! Hansard squinted down his nose and smiled grimly.

"That's the ticket!" he said softly. "I thought somehow or other he'd manage to get back. I wonder if it's two canoes or one? Heavens! I hope it's only one. What an infernal time he takes to come in sight! He's taking it pretty easy this morning. Pretty hot out there in mid-stream, I s'pose."

And then Dahamin came suddenly into sight. As Hansard had surmised, he was not exerting himself to any great extent. Occasionally he would withdraw the paddle from the water altogether and let the boat drift on its way as far as the current would allow.

"Seems pretty miserable," remarked the planter to himself. "Guess he's had a rough time of it overnight. Jove, but I'd give anything for a bottle of nice cool beer."

The canoe drew nearer, and then Hansard noticed that the Dusun was singing softly to himself—a chant so weird and unearthly that it startled the hidden listener.

"Sounds like a beastly funeral dirge," he said.

The sun shone suddenly on to the blade of the *parang* in the bottom of the boat, and for the time the flash of refracted light obscured everything else.

Hansard whistled. "He went out with very sanguine intentions," he thought. "I mustn't let the beggar get a look in first with that. I expect it's as keen as a razor."

Suddenly Dahamin stood upright in the boat and held his paddle aloft.

"I am Dahamin!" he shouted in Malay. "I am the

trader, the head-hunter, the feared of all races. I have taken heads in war; I am a man when others are slaves!"

Hansard stared open-mouthed at his enemy. There was a wild glare in the Dusun's eye that he feared to meet. He could not understand this sudden outburst on the part of the usually silent Dahamin. The canoe drifted slowly in to shore, but the trader did not try to stop it or turn it once more into mid-stream. By some curious chance Fate was bringing Hansard his enemy—bringing him to the very spot where the planter lay hidden.

And then, as the canoe grounded on the soft soil of the bank, Dahamin stooped down to the boat and raised something aloft. "See!" he shouted hoarsely to the wilds, "no white hand can ever vanquish me! My arm is too strong for them, my sight too keen, my aim too sure! I took a white head and they hunted me down; now another white head has fallen to a blow of my trusty *parang*!"

And as the savage chanted his war-cry to the jungle and the river, Hansard saw and understood. His horrified gaze fell on the distorted features of the only friend in his solitude. Mad with rage and grief, he grasped his hunting-knife, and, springing like a wild cat from the undergrowth, buried the long blade deep between the Dusun's shoulders.

Dahamin uttered a queer gurgling cry, coughed horribly, and fell like a log into the stream, the knife still protruding from his back. Hansard staggered back and sat heavily down, passing a hand wearily over his fevered brow. It had all happened so suddenly. Had he really taken life—human life? It had seemed so easy, so ridiculously simple. Just one blow, and that was all.

He covered his eyes with his hands for a moment and then looked up. "Poor old Mellor!" he said, and started scraping a hole in the ground with the blade of Marani's *kris*. He felt no qualms as he lifted the detective's head from the moored canoe and buried it in solitude beneath the shade of the sheltering palms.

"Anyhow," he murmured, as he pressed the earth down with his roughly-sandalled foot, "he died in action and was not unavenged."

He hid the canoe in the reeds by the river's bank in case the dark-eyed Marani should wander that way seeking her father. The body of the Dusun trader had floated out into deep water before it sank, carrying with it all traces of the tragedy. And so it happened that, by a curious kink in the world's affairs, Mellor, the brave, the circumspect, the necessarily sober, armed with a six-chambered revolver and backed by a deep knowledge of the wilds, failed to overcome the man he had tracked to his lair; while Hansard, the weak-willed and dissolute, had raised his hand but once and the dreaded Dahamin breathed no more.

The planter turned suddenly on his heel and made his way back to the part of the bank near the clearing where he had been accustomed to sit and idly smoke the tropic mornings away. He did not know how near he had been that day to the trader's secret store, for, wild with exultation, a sudden desire for a sip of intoxicating liquor had caused Dahamin to let his craft drift to the bank nearest the place where his wares were concealed.

"To-night"—he said to himself, feeling for his pipe—"to-night I will elude Marani, steal down to where the canoe is hidden, and push out into the stream. I shall paddle down the river as well as I can and chance my luck with the snags. Marani must look out for herself, and she's not likely to live alone for long. Anyhow, I must consider Dorothy before her. I shall have the only boat there is now, and, Dahamin being dead, I have nothing to fear. Poor old Mellor! His luck was out last night with a vengeance."

Marani was singing at her work, laughing inwardly at the coming trap she had prepared for Hansard— the bottle of fiery spirit she had hidden in the house where she could lay her hand on it without his knowledge.

"When it is evening," she told herself, "he will come to me for company, as all human creatures seek companionship before the darkness hides the earth. Under my sarong shall I hide the bottle, ready opened, the broad, flat cork but loosely pressed into its place. I will place it on the floor by his side while he is thoughtful. He is as helpless as a little child when there is anything good to drink."

She clapped her hands suddenly and called to him.

"*Mari! Mari-sini, tuan! Mahu makan?* (Do you want anything to eat?)"

Hansard appeared from the trees on the farther side of the clearing and shook his head. "*Tida* (no)," he said. "It is too hot, and I am not well."

Marani appeared concerned.

"*Panus-panus, tuan*?" (Fever), she asked, looking up from her work.

He crossed towards her, and, taking her in his arms, kissed her passionately on the lips.

"We shall have to be good friends now," he said, "we two."

Marani started and looked up into his eyes, as if trying to fathom what was behind them.

"We two? Good friends? What does the white *tuan* mean?"

Hansard bit his thumb-nail and stammered. He had in a weak moment said more than he had meant to say.

"Perhaps your father will never return," he replied slowly.

Her face grew solemn.

"He will come back," she whispered. "He is so brave and so clever."

Hansard released her and went into the hut to sleep. As the atmosphere cooled he went back to the jungle to make final preparations for his departure. He found fruit—bananas, green oranges, and a juicy *pomolo*—and, tying them in a cloth, threw them into the canoe. "At midnight I shall be well on my way," he said, and went back to spend a last fleeting hour or two with the beautiful dark daughter of the late trader, Dahamin.

Insects hummed in the evening air. Wonderful lights shone in the sky—heliotrope and orange and red. A stag coughed, and monkeys quarrelled ceaselessly in the branches above.

Hansard and Marani sat on the floor by the door of the hut waiting for the fall of darkness.

"Night!" remarked Hansard suddenly.

"Yah," replied Marani sleepily, and guided his hand to where a round earthenware bottle stood at his side.

"I am thirsty," she whispered, "but the white *tuan* must drink first—not too deeply, though, for there is not much left in the bottle for two."

The planter pushed the bottle aside, and, putting his arms round her, turned his head deliberately away from temptation.

"No," he said fiercely, "I shall never taste *samsu* again. It is accursed liquor!"

Marani fixed her dark eyes on his and kissed him passionately. Her sudden display of affection thrilled him. Hitherto she had only lain in his arms, submitting to his caresses.

"Very well," he cried, "we'll just drink a cup to your health, Marani! It's been deuced hot to-day."

The last sentence he added as a kind of excuse to silence a warning voice within him.

An hour later Hansard lay on the floor of the hut snoring like a pig. Forgotten was his wife, his home at Limana, the canoe drawn up in the bushes waiting for him.

Marani dragged him to the native mat where he slept and lay down beside him. "The locket is mine," she said softly, "when I can take it from him." She unbuttoned his tattered coat, found the clip which fastened the two ends of gold chain, and drew the precious locket from his neck.

And Hansard, oblivious of everything, snored on.

VI. THE SPIRIT OF VENDETTA

MARANI LAY AWAKE FOR HOURS by Hansard's side listening to the loud breathing of the drunken planter. Outside was the inky darkness, the ghost-infested jungle—the very masses of foliage resembling shrouded forms to the imaginative eye! Creatures of the night prowled near at hand; huge apes moved in the branches; stags thrust the boughs aside and uttered their cough-like signal to their mates. The dark Dusun girl felt strangely alone that night. She had been accustomed to the desolate beyond from her very childhood, and had long been used to finding her way quickly and fearlessly in dark places; and yet to-night she was afraid! Afraid of what? She did not quite know, but whenever she closed her eyes to await the slumber natural to the healthy animal, a vague vision came before her eyes, only to be dispelled by quickly opening them again.

In sheer desperation she determined to avert her attention from what she at that moment most desired, and hoped that by thinking of other matters Nature, in her contrariness, might grant her sleep. The first thought that occupied her mind was her father, Dahamin—the trader upon whose head there was a price—whom the police had sought for years in vain. More than a day had passed since he left in the old, frail canoe to pursue the stranger who had

disappeared with his newer vessel. What could have
delayed him? she wondered. Skilled in the use of the
paddle as he was, he could not have taken long to
draw level with his enemy.

Supposing—A terrible thought crossed her mind,
and she shuddered involuntarily. Supposing he had
failed, and the other man had managed to—strike
first? Supposing her father were even now lying
dead, deep in the waters of the lonely river? She sat
up cross-legged on the rough mat, the greater half of
which the drunken Hansard monopolized, and
rocked to and fro, moaning softly to herself all the
while. If Dahamin were indeed dead—if he should
never again return to the little hut in the clearing by
the stream—what would become of her? She buried
her head in her hands and tried hard to pierce the
curtain of the future. What would become of her?
She turned suddenly and gazed at the snoring form
at her side. For all his faults, she liked this weak,
handsome white man whom her father had brought
to their house months before lest he should tell the
authorities of the trader's whereabouts. And, after
all, loathsome as he was under the influence of the
deadly Chinese *samsu*, the fault lay partly with herself, who had played upon his weakness and put the
liquor in his way in order to attain her own ends.

If Dahamin did not return, her future existence
seemed pretty clearly mapped out. There was now
no canoe, and so, unless he roused himself from his
slothfulness and made one, Hansard could never run
away from her. He was far too inexperienced to dare
to risk a perilsome journey on foot through all those
dreary miles of dense jungle, deadly swamp, and

widespread *padi*-lands. Hansard and she would love and live as best they could together. He could not trade as her father had done and bring her luxuries from the villages and towns he visited. He could only gather fruit, and perhaps might learn to trap birds and small animals. The future did not seem to promise very much. Dahamin had been wont to buy her bright trinkets when his business had gone well—silver anklets and bangles—and once he had given her gold earrings, such as the Tamil women love, and little studs of the same precious metal to ornament each side of her broad nose. Hansard was far too poor now to give her anything.

Suddenly she started and passed one dark hand round her neck. The fine gold chain which held the locket she had stolen from the planter was still where she had placed it. It was a beautiful little trinket, she thought, more valuable than anything she had ever possessed before. Supposing he should awake and miss it, and demand it from her again? Should she hide it in the woods, and mark the place so that she might know it again? She could not understand why he valued it—such ornaments were not designed for white men's wearing. He had flown into a furious temper when she had discovered it hanging round his sun-burnt neck, and had told her she could have it—"when she could get it!" Well, she had got it now! She had exerted all her native cunning, made him drunk with fermented liquor, and taken it from him while he slept! That was all fair enough, she argued to herself; and white men are not infrequently admirers of fair play. He had made no definite rules for the game; had issued no instructions for her to adhere to. He had simply stated that she could have it when she could get it. She *had* obtained it—by her own methods—and in all fairness there was nothing more to be said.

Hansard snored on, and Marani crept softly to the little hole in the wall which served for a door in this queer mushroom-like homestead, and gazed out into the night. Clouds obscured the moon, and soon a breeze sprang up, shaking the branches, whistling in the reeds by the river, and bringing with it a heavy shower of pelting raindrops which rattled like a score of kettle-drums on the sago-leaf roof above.

"*Hujan* (rain)!" she murmured. "It will be cooler and more pleasant after, and perhaps I shall be able to sleep. *Bi-la*! I *am* so tired—and he snores like a *babi* (pig)! I shall be glad when it is day again."

The pattering ceased on the *atap* roof, and a queer, grey, ghostly light crept into the clearing—an apologetic envoy sliding into the Court of the Queen of Night to gently break the news that the Sun King would presently come to drive her from her dominions.

Marani shivered, and drew the shawl more tightly over her shoulders. It would not be long now before dawn. Suddenly she started and craned her head forward, striving to pierce the gloom. Something seemed to be flapping down there in the clearing, like a torn sarong on a line. She racked her brains trying to remember whether she had left anything hanging to dry—a native mat, perhaps, or a shawl? She looked back over her shoulder at Hansard, and when her gaze travelled back once more to the clearing the flapping she had noticed seemed to have moved to the other side—nearer the river! She rubbed her eyes and looked again, trying to detect something about it that might give her a clue to its identity. What could it be out there in the first faint grey light of early dawn? And then there came back to her memory of the blurred vision she had seen on closing her eyes a few hours before. It had seemed as if a shapeless, shrouded form were beckoning to her—ever beckoning. Down in the clearing the thing still motioned monotonously, but a second time its position seemed changed!

She looked back at Hansard again, but his great form lay sprawling over the native mat, and he still snored noisily.

She opened her mouth to scream, but terror gripped her, and she could not utter a sound. There was a shadowy, shapeless figure standing at the foot of the rickety bamboo ladder which led up to the little doorway where she crouched—and an arm, like a pillar of fog, beckoned to her to come. Thrusting her head into the crook of her arm, like a schoolboy ducking to avoid a threatening blow, she waited—waited for she knew not what. She dared not think what this strange visitation might signify. In her primitive line of thought she fancied it must be some evil spirit of the jungle luring her, perhaps, to her doom while yet the earth was partly cloaked in darkness. Perhaps it was a sign to warn her to keep within doors during the hours of night, and not seek to pry into the secrets of the blackness without. Raising her head timidly the fraction of an inch, she peeped out over her arm. The form had vanished!

She laughed hysterically, and smoothed down the folds of her sarong with both hands.

"I was dreaming," she said. "It is foolish to sit here in the chill air of early morning—perhaps I shall have fever. *Apah ito* (what's that)?"

Down at the very edge of the jungle, exactly opposite the spot where she sat, a bright light appeared suddenly between the trees, like a great firefly, only—it was stationary! It glowed like a live coal, so brightly that Marani longed to discover its origin.

"I am *honto* (bewitched)!" she sobbed softly. "I can only see strange things to-night!"

But whereas the beckoning form in the clearing had frightened her, this new vision seemed to have the exactly opposite effect. It fascinated her. She sat suddenly upright, then rose to her feet, stooped to avoid knocking her head on the top of the low doorway, descended the rickety ladder slowly and deliberately till she reached the ground, and crossed towards where the strange light showed between a coco-palm and a jack-fruit tree.

As she advanced towards it the spark of light moved just so many paces away—like a will-o'-the-wisp; but still she hastened after it beyond the clearing, beyond a strip of dense jungle, and along the river's bank. It led suddenly through a belt of trees and then disappeared. She stood for a moment by the water side, trying to see which direction the strange light had taken. The dawn was rising in the east, and the jungle trees stood out like giant wraiths from the early morning's mist, which hovered just above the earth.

Marani began to feel very lonely again out there all alone in the half-light. Why had the figure beckoned to her and the light led her so strangely from her home? And why had she been so foolish as to follow? She must hurry back and try to get some sleep before Hansard woke and wanted breakfast.

She turned to retrace her steps, when something bright, gleaming through the rank reeds by the riverside, attracted her attention. It shone in the growing light like polished metal. She stepped forward and parted the reeds with both hands, and looked into the water. For a moment she gazed at a lifeless mass in silent horror; then, uttering a wild peal of hysterical laughter, rushed madly from the scene—through the jungle, and back into the clearing. She threw herself at full length on the soft ground and sobbed as though her heart would break.

She had seen the lifeless corpse of her father, half submerged in the stream, a long, keen hunting knife imbedded between his dark shoulder-blades!

Dahamin had fallen at last—he had set out on his long last chase—his head-hunting was over for ever. It seemed to her as if an earthquake had chanced upon her small world and wrecked it from the very foundation. Her castles in the air were shattered, and their flimsy structure came tumbling down upon her head as she lay and sobbed—oblivious of everything but her new great sorrow.

An hour later she rose suddenly and dried her eyes on her sarong. A hard, determined look had come into her face, and there would be no more weeping for Dahamin after this. Had she lived in Corsica, she would have recognized that there was in embryo within her heaving bosom the fierce spirit of merciless vendetta. Her father had met his death unprepared—stabbed from behind by some ruthless, unknown enemy. Whose was this queer knife, the like of which she never remembered seeing before? Could it be the work of a white man? That seemed improbable, for she had heard that white men carry weapons which kill from afar off—and yet the knife, at the first glance, had looked too finished for a weapon of native manufacture. She endeavoured, in her primitive way, to reconstruct the scene of Dahamin's death? it meant everything to her, this sudden bereavement; and the shock of it served to brighten her forest-dulled intellect and to open up a hitherto unused cell in her brain.

Dahamin had set forth early the night before; his enemy, in a new canoe, half an hour ahead of him. Inch by inch she pictured it; the old canoe had gained on the new one, propelled, no doubt, by a far less experienced hand. At last, panting with the great exertion, the men in the vessels had drawn level; weapons had flashed in the light of the moon, and then—She paused in her wild flight of imagination, and remembered the most vital point in the whole case. If the thief who had stolen the canoe from the rushes had been the assassin, how came it that he had surprised and killed the trader so near his own home, without the slightest sound of the conflict reaching her listening ears? Dahamin had been surprised near the clearing. He must, then, have given up the chase and returning to her. Had the thief stolen back without the cunning trader noticing his presence on the river? It seemed absurd! Perhaps there was more than one man watching her movements? Yet she had only noticed one, and had called her father's attention to the presence of a spy.

She hastened back towards the spot where she had left the body lying half-submerged. All fear of looking on the dead had forsaken her now, and, suddenly endowed with the instincts of a sleuth-hound, she was determined to smell out the trail, using every piece of evidence at her disposal. She stopped halfway and lifted both beautiful arms above her. And the deep, dark jungle, the winding river, the rustling reeds, and the blue heavens, now laughing in the light of the rising tropic sun, bore witness to a solemn oath shouted hoarsely in their hearing alone. Her beautiful face was contorted with the frenzy of a Mullah, her arms writhed sinuously to the overflowing of her passion. She hissed like a beautiful creature of the jungle, and, with lithe, determined movements, stepped onwards towards her destination.

"The sleep of night shall be my only rest until I have found him and compassed his death!"

That was the vow all nature heard, and the great wild climbing things rustled sympathetically. Nature was in accord with the mental anguish of her true-born child.

Marani, forcing her way through the tall, rank grass by the riverside, came suddenly upon the canoe, noted its blood-stained bottom, and cast a shrewd, comprehending glance over the blow-pipe, the deadly poisoned arrows, and the recently-moistened blade.

"Then my father killed the man he sought," she said. "He returned with his head—for there is blood in the boat!"

She opened the bamboo cylinder and noted how many of the darts had been expended.

"If my father slew his foe and returned from the fight, fearing nothing, whose was the hand that struck him suddenly down?"

She wrinkled her brow, and crept in search of the trader's body, following the river's bank for more than half a mile—but the corpse was nowhere to be found!

"It has drifted with the stream," she said. "It is as well; perhaps. He was supreme on the great waters; he knew them as no other man has done—it is meet that he should sleep his last sleep in their embrace."

She stood for a while gazing down into the stream, and then she opened her eyes wide and thought.

"Hansard!" Could it be he? Where, if so, had he obtained the knife? She remembered, too, another thing, which up to now had escaped her attention. When he had gone from her angry at her interest in the golden locket, she had heard the rattle of steel on steel at his side. She knew the planter had her own weapon, for had he not wrenched it from her before he kissed her?

"I will find out soon," she hissed, and, noting carefully where the canoe lay concealed, stole back to the clearing and the hut where Hansard still snored.

"I must wait," she whispered, peering in at the tiny doorway. "While he yet sleeps there are important things to consider. I must not forget that he is a man, strong and armed—ah!"

She crept stealthily across the rough-boarded floor to where he lay. His arms were spread out widely apart, one half resting on the wall of the hut, the other partly on the matting and partly on the floor itself. The tattered khaki coat he always wore possessed now but one button—a removable affair, secured by means of a blunted safety-pin of white metal. Deftly she pressed the white button through the torn-out buttonhole and passed her hand lightly over his leathern belt. "A serpent is powerless when deprived of its sting," she hissed; "and a wild cat, as he called me once, is dangerous while yet her claws are sharp."

The black hands scarcely trembled as she fumbled with the sharp *kris* at his side.

Hansard stirred and rolled suddenly over on to his face. She started hastily back and turned, as if seeking some article of household use required for preparing the morning's meal. The planter grunted, mumbled something in English she could not understand, and then snored again with renewed vigour. She turned towards him once more, and saw that the weapon she sought was now under his heavy form. She cursed softly, and spat out of the doorway into the clearing.

"It is not an easy thing," she muttered. "The effects of the *samsu* cannot last for ever. Perhaps even now, at the slightest disturbance, he will wake—and still be dangerous."

She crept close up to him once more and threw both her arms round his neck. He stirred slightly, but did not open his eyes. Slowly the dark hands travelled from his neck to his shoulders, from his shoulders to his sides, until at last the supple fingers sought the place in his belt where the sharp-edged *kris* was thrust. Her right hand rested on the handle; her left held the belt securely in its place. A sharp pull, and the weapon came a few inches in her grasp; in a moment it would be hers again, the wild cat would have its claws, and knew full well how to use them. The sleeper moved again, and groaned.

Marani remained where she was, lying very still, and scarcely daring to breathe. Suddenly she started and sat up. Hansard, still asleep, was talking in queer, short sentences, in a language she did not understand. Then she recognized a few words in crude Malay. At last she caught whole sentences in the tongue she understood, and, with beating heart, she listened intently, eagerly taking in every syllable that was spoken.

"I must go home—go home at once! Dahamin, you *kiti*! I've been here too long already—much too long. They'll think I'm dead by now. Never mind, we'll surprise them this time. Turn the boat round, I say—turn her round at once—do you hear me? I want to go back—down the river again. Crocodiles? I'm not afraid of crocodiles now! You saved my life once from crocodiles—I paid you, didn't I? Yes, I paid you, you thief! Boot's on different foot now, you know—on different foot altogether! Pretty daughter—Marani, eh?—too pretty to be your daughter—much too pretty. She can't help you now, though. I've taken her *kris*! Turn the boat round, will you? You know the river—I don't. How long to get to Limina? Must get back soon—"

Marani drank in every word, listened carefully to the incoherent, purposeless gabble which punctuated every few sentences, hoping against hope that sooner or later he would murmur something incriminating. A huge spider ran across the floor, but she heeded it not. Outside, in the clearing, the sun was casting huge shadows from the trees, and a woodpecker tapped somewhere behind the house. Had a snake wound its sinuous course within a yard of her she could not have stirred. The rambling, disjointed murmur commenced again.

"So you won't, eh? Don't want to turn back. I say you must—you shall—see? I must go home at once. Marani—yes, she's pretty—very pretty—but I must forget all about her—now—too important business—what? Not afraid of me? Unarmed! You don't know—I've got a damn sharp *kris*, and—"

A branch fell noisily on the *atap* roof, and the sleeper stopped abruptly. Hansard raised himself on one elbow, turned over on his side, and then lay down again. Marani could have wept from sheer rage and annoyance. It was just her luck that the planter should have been disturbed at a time when something interesting appeared to be about to follow.

"So you've killed him, have you?" Hansard began.

Marani sat very still, great beads of perspiration standing out on her dark forehead, her heart beating wildly.'

"Poor old Mellor's dead—dead—and you've killed him—head's there in the boat, eh? Good friend to me. Another white man you've killed, you blackguard! Turn the boat round! No more *samsu*— never again—too much already—live a sober life now—ah!—"

With a wild cry Hansard suddenly rolled on to his back, sat up, and opened his eyes very wide. A strong hand clutched the dark wrist which held the sharp *kris*, and the weapon fell harmlessly to the floor. He gazed sleepily at the frightened girl by his side.

"Marani!" he cried hoarsely. "So you tried to get some of your own back, did you? You sly devil! You're not smart enough for me, you know."

His free hand went suddenly to his side.

"Jove!" he said, "what's become of my hunting-knife?"

Marani uttered a shrill scream and, wrenching her arm from his grasp, sprang like a tigress at his throat. Hansard caught both her wrists once more and tore her hands from his neck, her sharp nails gouging tiny holes in the flesh, so that the blood ran in little streams on to his coat.

"Are you mad?" he cried hoarsely, and, rising suddenly to his feet, threw her with great force into a far corner, where she lay still, panting like a wild creature of the forest, baffled but as yet uncon-quered.

"I must keep a close eye on you, Marani," he re-marked, fastening the only button his tattered jacket could boast, and slipping the sharp *kris* securely back into its place. "So it was all a clever little trick, your making love to me yesterday, eh? By heaven! I believe you'd have murdered me in cold blood. Eh, what's that?"

The girl had muttered something beneath her breath, which she did not repeat when challenged.

Suddenly he remembered something, and his hand sought his neck, still bleeding from the wounds her nails had made. The warm colour surged into his cheeks beneath the tan, his brows contracted with sudden fury.

"The locket, you she-devil! Where is the locket I wore when I fell asleep last night?"

His eye caught the empty *samsu* bottle by the doorway, and he knew.

"So you drugged me with that poison?" he said slowly, advancing a pace towards her. "You meant to have that pretty gew-gaw by hook or by crook, fair means or foul! Well, I promised you you should have it if you could get it—and you've had it in your possession some time now, I suppose. But if you and I have got to live together here there's got to be a better understanding than this. There's only going to be one boss here—and that's me. *Tahu?*"

With a swift movement he unbuckled his belt and crossed the floor towards her. Seizing her arm he dragged her into the centre of the room and ripped her brightly-coloured sarong from top to bottom. Then he raised his arm and rained heavy blows on her naked back. Marani writhed as the leather belt rose and fell, then burst out sobbing and bit at his wrist with her sharp teeth. With an oath he loosened his grasp, and Marani ran suddenly from the hut, down the rickety bamboo ladder, across the clearing, and into the jungle beyond.

Hansard watched her disappear, a grim smile playing on his bearded face.

"Damn demoralizing!" he said. "And I hated doing it—but it just had to be. If I don't keep her well in hand she'll murder me one night in my sleep. Jove! the little devil's got long nails!"

He passed his hand once more over his lacerated neck, and sank into a sitting posture on the floor. Presently, feeling hungry, he searched the house until he found a ripe pomolo as big as a water melon. He tore it quickly open, and the acid juice cooled his burning palate. He consumed this and a couple of green bananas, and then found his bamboo pipe and pouch of fibrous tobacco.

"Lord!" he ejaculated, as the blue smoke curled roofwards, "I let myself go again last night and spoiled still another chance of escape. As likely as not she'll prowl round and discover where I've hidden the canoe. One thing's certain—I must make up my mind once for all that if I am never sober in my life again, I must be so this evening. Everything depends on it. In the cool of the afternoon I shall start on my journey, and with good luck should be home again by to-morrow night at the latest. I shan't be at all sorry either. I've had just about enough of this."

Marani did not stop running until she reached the trader's hidden storehouse back in the jungle near where the canoe lay concealed. Here she found herself a fresh sarong and a coat of black velvet, fastening in front by means of three huge silver brooches.

Clothed once more, but still smarting from the heavy blows of Hansard's strap, she busily made preparations for a hurried departure.

"He took my father's life," she said. "Before the evening is come I shall have taken his in return."

She filled a spare sarong with fruit and a bottle of water, and secured it by knotting the four corners together. Everything ready for her flight, she lay down in the rushes by the river's bank and waited patiently for the sun to sink in the heavens. The day wore slowly on, and the shadows grew longer, until at last the girl rose to her feet, and, running the canoe down into the water, seized the paddle and stepped lightly in. She paddled well out into the stream, and then stooped to pick up the deadly *sumpitan*. She slipped a poisonous arrow into the tube and waited. Then she cried out in a shrill, mocking voice, which echoed in the vast stillness:

"Tuan! Tu-an! Mari-sini!"

There was a long pause and then she called again:

"Tuan—Tu-an, sihaya pergi!"

A sound of heavy footsteps down the jungle path, the noise of a heavy form passing quickly through the undergrowth, a bellow of rage, and Hansard, purple in the face and panting furiously, stood on the river's bank opposite the girl in the canoe; barely a dozen yards between them.

Marani stood very erect in the boat, the long bamboo tube in one hand.

"Tuan," she cried, "I know that you slew my father when his back was turned. I know that you intended to run away and leave me alone here in the loneliness of the jungle—unarmed. Now, O White

Tuan, the tables are turned. I am going to leave you here, where white man's foot has scarcely ever trod; but I will be merciful—I will at least see that you do not live too long to suffer in silence and alone."

Swiftly the bamboo tube rose to her lips, she drew a deep breath, and, within a fraction of a second, the deadly arrow was on its way shorewards. Like a flash it sped with almost miraculous sureness, and Hansard, uttering one wild cry of despair, crashed heavily to the ground.

Marani tossed the tube and the remaining arrows overboard, and turned her canoe's head down the stream.

With a weird, triumphant shout, which startled the very monkeys in the riverside trees, she raised the paddle and drove it dexterously into the water.

VII. THE LADY OF THE LOCKET

THE LONG CANOE sped swiftly down the stream, bringing Marani from the way-back home she had known so long towards a comparative civilization of which she as yet knew scarcely anything. Her father was dead, and the white man who had compassed his death lay even now on the river's bank, a poisoned arrow—warranted to take life in ten seconds—piercing his flesh. She was rather surprised at herself, for she felt neither sadness for her father's untimely end, nor any qualms of conscience that the murder of the Englishman Hansard lay at her door. The lion does not weep nor worry over the lamb it has recently slain. Marani, wild creature of the forest that she was, possessed the usual characteristics of wild creatures generally. If stroked and humoured, she could be pleasant; if crossed or wounded, her dark eyes flashed fire and her whole being was exerted to compass her revenge.

To-day, seated in the broad canoe which she had taken the previous afternoon before Hansard could prevent her, Marani's mind was quite at ease, and when her arm grew tired she would dangle her dark fingers over the side until they dipped into the stream, humming all the while a queer little air of her own. This new journey of a few short miles was as wonderful to her as a trip round the world is to the average Englishmen. Every new feature in the landscape pleased her, and she clapped her hands delightedly when the jungle ceased suddenly and the wide, open stretch of *padi*-lands began. This was adventure—real, stirring adventure. She had passed many crocodiles thrusting their snouts above the river, or lying motionless like fallen tree-trunks on the sloping banks. An enormous red-haired orang-outang had snarled at her, crouching high up in a riverside tree, and a flock of rhino-birds had varied the monotony of a long straight stretch of water.

Her glance fell upon the sharp, curved *parang* at her feet in the bottom of the canoe. If need were, she could defend herself, for had she not taken the life of a man—a white man—one of an all-conquering, all-subduing race? What a pity it was that in that one superb moment of exultation at seeing her enemy fall she had thrown the deadly arrows and tube into the water! Had she but kept them she might even kill a monkey to vary the monotony of meals, which consisted solely of fruit. It is a curious fact that the deadly poison into which the natives of Borneo dip their arrows, although it brings instant death on piercing the flesh, yet leaves the body wholesome, and animals killed by its aid can afterwards be eaten by the hunter with impunity.

The river was getting broader now, and there were fewer bends in its course. The jungle, too, was not so high as that she had just left behind her, and there were more open spaces and *padi*-fields. Late in the afternoon a tall mountain appeared suddenly and un-expectedly to her right, and a ridge of low hills ex-tended from either bank of the river apparently to infinity. Marani rested her paddle on her knees and sucked her thumb thoughtfully.

There was what appeared to be a fairly large squat house on the top of one of the near-lying hills, and the trees which covered the slopes were set at regular intervals. Suddenly she passed under a rough bamboo bridge, and a fat Chinaman in white ducks, and a white pith sun-helmet set at a rakish angle on his head, leered at her, and shouted to her to stop a moment and talk with him.

Marani would have liked to see the frail structure give way and pitch him headlong into the water. She laughed aloud at the picture her imagination had conjured up—the wretched yellow-skinned, overfed youth scrambling from the water and eyeing his ruined suit of ducks ruefully. The Chinaman heard the sudden peal of mirth and mistook it for a challenge to him to follow. He left the bridge and ran after her down the path by the bank. *"Tabi!"* he shouted, but Marani did not even vouchsafe him a glance. The young man ran still faster, tripped suddenly, and fell headlong on to the soft earth of the river's bank. By the time he had recovered his feet again and paused to dust himself down the dark-eyed witch in the old canoe was far out of sight. He rammed his topi still farther over one eye, lit a cheap cigarette, and strolled up a narrow path towards the adjacent rubber estate.

"Pretty girl!" he told himself. "I wonder what she's doing in that boat and where she comes from? She led me a nice dance, anyhow."

The canoe skimmed lightly through the water, past a village of queer little huts all standing well out of the water on long poles. Women seated on the steps or at their miniature doorways called after her and laughed as she passed by in silence. Men paused in their daily toil to watch the boat until it had passed from view round a sharp bend, and little naked children ran some way after her, whooping delightedly.

Darkness fell suddenly, and Marani paddled her frail bark shorewards. She stepped lightly on to the bank, drew the canoe up after her, and sat down to discuss her evening meal. She threw the skins of the fruit into the river and turned to discover a suitable tree in which she might spend the night in safety. She walked a hundred yards and paused to survey her surroundings as best she could. The moon stole suddenly out from behind a bank of clouds, and Marani started back as she almost collided with a dark form coming in the opposite direction. The stranger was taller than those of her race, and wore a turban and a short black beard. His coat was of a cut similar to the khaki jacket Hansard had always worn, and a coloured sarong descended from under it down to his knees.

She caught her breath and turned aside to avoid him, but he had seen her as soon as she had noticed him, and followed her.

"*Siapa kau?* (who are you?)" he demanded in Malay.

"My name is Marani," she said simply.

"What are you doing alone in the darkness so far from any village?"

She racked her brains. Somehow or other she must escape this strange man. There was something about him she instinctively mistrusted. He was standing right in front of her now and she saw that he carried a heavy cane.

"I was visiting a friend," she almost whispered, "and darkness overtook me. I have lost my way and cannot discover my boat. Also I am very frightened."

The stranger laughed—an evil laugh—and Marani wished she had remembered to bring the sharp *parang* with her.

"Listen!" she cried hoarsely. "What was that?"

"I hear nothing," replied the man. "There is wind in the trees to-night, that is all."

"Ah," she sighed deeply, "I am so tired!"

The stranger's black arm slipped suddenly round her lissom waist, and a hot, bearded face was thrust against her own.

"I have a comfortable house *sana* (over there)," he said. "There is room for two there. Tahu? It will be better than a night in the open, and I have a warm supper waiting for me."

The moon was hidden again and Marani resolved to make a speedy dash for freedom before it was too late. She glanced hastily round her—the nearest belt of trees was a hundred yards and more away.

"Yah!" she murmured resignedly, submitting to his embrace, "I will come. It is cold out here in the early morning, and there is fever near the water. Look! Ah, see, there is a snake in the path. Your stick, *lakas!* (quickly!)"

"A snake! Where?" The tall stranger released her suddenly, and advanced half a dozen paces in the

direction she indicated, his stick firmly grasped in
his right hand, his shoulders bent low.

Marani turned on her heel and fled as fast as her
legs would carry her to where her canoe lay hidden
in the rank grass by the bank. The tall Sikh—for
such the stranger was—took but a moment to perceive how easily he had been duped, and with an
oath ran swiftly after her. At the very water's edge
he drew level with her and seized her by the arm.

"Not so fast, my pretty one," he sneered. "So you
thought to avoid me thus easily? Well, you have yet
to learn how poorly one is repaid for deception in
this world."

He caught her up in his strong arms and was about
to hasten homewards with his newfound plaything,
when something bright on her neck attracted his
gaze. He let her slip to the ground once more and
made a sudden grab at the fine gold chain. It
snapped at a weak link, and the Sikh stepped back-
wards a couple of short paces, holding before him
the golden locket and chain she had stolen from
Hansard while he lay in a drunken slumber.

"It is English make," he gasped, "and worth many
dollars. Tell me—where did you get it?"

He had not noticed a dark hand slipping over the
side of a hidden canoe. He thrust his outstretched
hand containing the ornament close to her face and
repeated the question.

"Where did you find this, you little Dusun thief?"

A sharp *parang* whistled suddenly through the air,
a cry of agony echoed in the stillness, and the Sikh,
shrieking, ran madly in circles for a brief space, and
then fell, his arm doubled under him. On the ground

where the moon-light played lay a dark hand, severed at the wrist, the fingers still closed over the
golden locket and chain. Marani paid no heed to the
poor wretch's howls, but, swiftly recovering her stolen property, pushed the canoe once more into the
water and was gone into the night.

"The wild cat has scratched again," she said.
"And it is time to seek a safer place where I may
sleep till dawn."

A mile farther down the river she landed once
more, and, climbing into a tall jack-fruit tree, discovered a place where several branches met, and
slept more or less comfortably until the bright light
of day woke her from her slumbers. Rubbing her
eyes, she slid down the stout trunk to the ground and
gazed at the landscape around her. Suddenly something unusual beneath her velvet coat caused her to
raise her hand to her neck. "He has broken the gold
ornament," she said, and undid the knot she had tied
where the chain was severed. The locket had opened
in the struggle, and within on one side under a piece
of glass was a lock of fair hair and on the other a
photograph of a beautiful, white-skinned woman.
Marani gazed at the first photograph her eyes had
ever seen in mute astonishment. It was, she knew,
the face of a woman—Hansard's wife, perhaps.
Now she knew why he had been so anxious to run
away and leave her alone in the wilds.

As she picked her way back to the canoe she
made one further resolve—she would devote herself
to discovering the identity of the woman Hansard
had so much admired. It would be some small con-

solation for Marani to wound her with the news of his death.

"She is very beautiful," she murmured, examining the portrait closely. Then she closed the locket and knotted the chain round her dark neck once more.

In a low hut in a hollow, *atap*-roofed and walled, a crippled form hovered over a large metal boiler, busily preparing the midday meal for a hundred and fifty toiling Chinese coolies. The man was young, and his features had been fine before some terrible affliction had lined his face and twisted his bones. A figure lounged up to the open door and, leaning heavily on the post, peered in.

"Tabi."

"Tabi."

The newcomer was an assistant at the *kedei* (shop) on the Limana Kabun, and had seized the opportunity of a slack half-hour to come across and have a chat with the crippled cook of No. 3 konzsie.

"How are you feeling this morning, Li-Hip-See?"

"As well as I shall ever be now," grumbled the bent Chinaman in a queer, wheezing voice. "I only hope that he who caused me all this pain endured it in a like measure before he died."

"It was a white man, was it not? I have, as you know, been here but a few weeks, but I have heard it said you were once strong and well—stronger than most of the coolies here."

Li-Hip-See lifted a hot lid by means of a piece of charred bamboo thrust beneath the handle and stirred the boiling contents of an enormous cauldron with a long stick.

"It was on a hot afternoon many months ago," he began. "I was hanging clothes to dry on the line outside that very bungalow up there on the hill. The manager was the *Tuan Besar* Hansard then—a drunken fool, who had a very beautiful wife, many times too beautiful and good for him. He had been drunk for weeks, scarcely ceasing to touch the liquor for two hours together. The afternoon was very still, and the dogs, I remember, were sleeping quietly beneath the house. Suddenly the manager came running from the verandah, shouting in a loud voice for his pony. I caught the beast on the hillside, where it had been running loose for some time, harnessed it, and led it towards him. I helped him mount and stepped quickly back to allow him to pass. What happened then I scarcely remember. Mad with drinking, he must have ridden straight at me, I fell heavily, a thousand hammers seemed to be pounding me to atoms, and I awoke to find myself in the rough hospital on the hillside—a cripple!"

"And the *tuan Besar?* (manager?)"

"Dead," replied the cook shortly. "How?" The *kedei* assistant was very interested.

"He rode into the jungle and was never seen again. His pony and harness were discovered some days later. His wife is now married again to a good man. You have heard of the *Tuan Besar* Bently? They tell me there is no master to equal him, and he is very rich."

"But supposing the other *tuan* is not dead?"

The cripple turned fiercely upon his companion. "He *is* dead!" he cried hoarsely. "He must be by now. Were he not, I would hunt him down from place to place until I found him, and then—then, weak as I am, I would find a way—"

A shadow fell across the floor, and a second form darkened the entrance. A beautiful dark Dusun woman stood before the two Chinamen, and her voice, when she addressed them in Malay, was very sweet.

"Tabi."

"Tabi."

"I have travelled far, and I am very hungry. Will you give me something to eat and a cup of fresh water, for my throat is parched?"

The crippled cook gazed at her in astonishment.

"Whence come you?" he demanded, eyeing her closely.

"Deri si-blas-sana (from right over there)," she replied, waving a plump arm vaguely to indicate the horizon. "I am alone," she added simply. "I have no father, and my mother I do not remember."

She approached the bent form by the cauldron and placed a hand on his shoulder.

"You have had much pain," she said sympathetically, "and it has rendered you kind-hearted and generous."

The crippled cook grunted, found a large enamelled plate, opened one of the saucepans, and ladled out a large helping of meat and rice. He handed her the food and a pair of wooden chop-sticks, which she regarded in amazement.

"I have never seen these before," she said at last.

"The other Chinaman whispered *"Nanti"* (wait), and ran across to the kedei, startling the hens pecking placidly in the dust outside the kitchen. He returned in a moment with a small bone spoon, and Marani greedily began shovelling hot rice into her mouth at a great rate.

She leaned back against the wall with a deep sigh, and thanked her host for his kindness. Suddenly the cripple's eye fell upon the knot in the gold chain at her neck.

"Gold!" he ejaculated, pointing with a finger possessing an overdeveloped nail.

Marani's brow darkened. This jewel she had so coveted, and at last stolen, seemed to have become a terrible nuisance to her in her new life. She untied the knot in the chain and opened the locket before the two Chinamen. Both peered eagerly at it over her shoulder.

Li-Hip-See dropped the stirring rod and snatched the locket from her hand.

"It is she!" he cried hoarsely. "It is she! Where did you get this? It must have been given to him by her—perhaps even yet the hoonoon lives. Where did you get this, woman?"

The young man from the kedei regarded his companion open-mouthed, but Marani only laughed aloud.

"A white *tuan* has given it me," she replied coolly.

"A white *tuan*! Tell me, is he still living?"

Marani eyed him roguishly. "Ah! little man," she laughed, "you would like to know my secrets so much."

The cripple was in no mood for joking. Behind him a cauldron lid rattled tumultuously, and boiling fluid ran bubbling down its metal side, but he heeded it not.

"Tell me," he repeated, quivering with emotion, "is the *Tuan* Hansard dead?"

Marani gazed out of the doorway into the sunlight.

"If I tell you," she asked, "will you take me to where this woman dwells whose picture I have here."

"Yah! that is easy, and I will do anything if you will but tell me!"

Marani half closed her eyes and surveyed him cunningly through the long lashes.

"I was healthy and strong before he came," said the cook. "His pony it was that trampled my form to what it is to-day. If he were not dead—"

"What then?"

"I would tear him limb from limb!" cried the cripple fiercely.

"Well, he is dead, little man."

The Chinaman's eyes sparkled. "Tell me, how did he die?" he asked.

"I slew him," replied Marani calmly, "because he killed my father."

"You killed him—you?"

"Yah; and stole that locket while he was yet warm."

The cripple's hands rubbed together, and he chuckled hoarsely. "I am avenged—nobly avenged!" he cackled. "You will stay with me, pretty one, and eat of my rice as long as it pleases you. There is always plenty of food here, for the manager of the estate whom I serve is generous."

"And when shall I see the white woman?"

"Listen! When the *Tuan* Hansard disappeared, his wife married another *tuan.* and even now these two are staying with the manager of this very kabun. When the darkness has fallen I will take you to a place from which you can see them on the lighted verandah. She is very beautiful, this lady."

Marani was thinking deeply. So Mrs. Hansard had married again! Perhaps there would be some reward due to her for removing Hansard out of the way of this new alliance? Who could tell? Anyhow, she must play her cards carefully, and in the meantime the crippled Li-Hip-See had offered her a home, and she was heartily sick of sleeping in the open and in trees!

"To-night, then, you will show me her?" she said, and followed him into an inner room.

At the fall of darkness Li-Hip-See led Marani towards the little bungalow on the hill-top.

A white-clad Kekil boy stood on a heavy wooden chair and lit the lamp which swung from the roof in the centre of the verandah.

"It seems almost a pity to have the light," said Dorothy Bently. "I love the dark nights out here— the stars always seem so much closer than they do at home, and the lanterns of belated travellers passing over the ridge look so pretty."

The manager of the Limana Kabun nodded and lit a cigar. Arthur Bently, who was already smoking, took a sip at a weak whisky-and-soda in a glass by his side.

"I'm afraid we've rather outstayed our welcome,

mine host," he said. "To-morrow we must return home again and resume work. I'm simply itching to be in harness."

The *tuan besar* laughed.

"Your husband is becoming far too avaricious, Mrs. Bently," he remarked. "Here he is—the wealthiest man out here, bar none, and he talks about itching to hurry back home and begin making more dollars! It's perfectly indecent! As for his ridiculous suggestion about outstaying your welcome—well, really, I must protest. When you leave me, I shall resume an existence of dull monotony until my leave comes round next year—unless, of course, someone chances to drop in for a night or two. It can be lonely out here, y'know."

"I *do* know," said Dorothy Bently suddenly, gazing into the darkness at the twinkling lights of a native trading vessel in the bay.

The two men exchanged glances, and smoked for a while in silence. Dorothy Bently, seated in her long chair on the verandah of a bungalow that had once been her home, recalled a memory of one dark period in her existence which had culminated in her first husband's disappearance. From this very verandah he had ridden to his doom.

Bently rose from his chair and crossed to her side. The manager muttered something about his dog, and went down the steps and round to the back of the house.

"Cheer up, little woman; it's all over and done with, long ago! Try not to remember it."

Her hand sought his, and she nestled her head against his white coat.

"It is foolish of me to think of that dreadful time," she said. "And you have been so kind, so devoted to me, since then, that I had almost forgotten I was ever married to him until this evening, when the trend of conversation carried my thoughts back against my will. Isn't it glorious out here?"

"Dorothy, before we leave this subject and try to forget it for ever, I would like to ask you one question—may I?"

"What is it, Arthur?"

"We have never had any definite proof that Hansard is dead."

"But his pony and harness—"

"I know all that, dear; but that is not a proof, it is merely a supposition. Of course, I don't for a moment doubt that he has snuffed out in the jungle long ago. But supposing he has not?"

Dorothy shuddered and uttered a cry of pain.

"Don't!" she whispered hoarsely. "It is too awful to think about—too terrible!"

"If he should come back and claim you—would you return to him?"

"Arthur! What do you mean?"

"I wish to know, dear—in the event of such a remote possibility occurring, you would have to choose between us—which would you choose. Don't be afraid of wounding me, dearest. You must have loved him to have ever married him."

Dorothy Bently rose from her chair, and, resting both her arms on his broad shoulders, looked straight into his eyes.

"I do not believe now I ever really loved him," she said. "You are the only man in this whole world

I could ever live with now! But please don't let's talk about it. Why should we trouble about what can never happen? Is it not enough that we are together, and happy?"

He drew her to him and kissed her forehead tenderly.

"I am sorry," he said. "Perhaps I am a trifle morbid to-night. I am so happy now with you that I cannot help feeling that it is all a dream and that one day I shall wake up to the stern realities of an enforced bachelor-dom!"

"You foolish old dear!" she cried, and sat down by his side as the boy came in for the glasses.

A woman's voice came suddenly out of the darkness from somewhere close at hand.

"Tabi, mem!"

"Who is there?" cried Bently, peering over the verandah rail.

"A Dusun woman would speak with the Mem Hansard," replied the voice.

Dorothy Bently gasped, and sat suddenly upright in her long cane chair. Who could this native woman be who addressed her by the name her first husband had given her?

"Come here," she said calmly, and Marani stepped on to the verandah and stood in the lamplight before them;

"What is your name?" demanded Bently, eyeing her sternly.

"Marani, *tuan*."

"Deri mana (where from)?"

"Sa-na, tuan." A black hand waved eloquently.

"What do you want with the Mem Bendy—and

why do you call her by another name?

Marani said nothing, but fumbled with something at her neck. She drew the locket from its place and held it out to Mrs. Bendy.

Dorothy took it from the woman, gazed at it, and turned very white. "It was his!" she gasped. "I gave it him years ago, and he wore it always."

Arthur Bently's jaw set firmly. That this unexpected event should have occurred almost immediately after his conversation with Dorothy seemed so extraordinary a coincidence that he was now prepared for any blow.

"Where did you get that?" he demanded sternly.

"A white *tuan* gave it me, *tuan.*"

Dorothy gasped. "He gave that to you?"

The girl nodded.

"He is alive, then?"

Marani did not answer. Bently advanced a step and shook her roughly by the shoulder.

"Speak, woman!" he cried hoarsely. "Is the man who gave you that locket dead—or alive?"

Marani raised her coal-black eyes and smiled, revealing two regular rows of perfect white teeth.

"You will buy this locket from me?" she asked calmly.

Bently thrust one hand into an upper pocket and threw a bundle of dollar notes on to the table. The girl grabbed them eagerly and thrust them into her sarong.

Dorothy Bently, her beautiful face lined with suspense, laid her hand kindly on the girl's black arm.

"Tell me what you know," she said softly.

From that moment Marani liked the beautiful

white lady of the locket.

"He—the *Tuan* Hansard—killed my father—and now he, too, is dead!"

Bently uttered a sigh of relief, and Dorothy sat down again, burying her face in her hands.

"You are sure of this?" asked Bently suddenly.

"Yah, *tuan*! I saw him fall with my own eyes, back there where few men are. It was a poisoned dart that pierced him, and he could not live after that."

Dorothy Bently shuddered.

"The *sumpitan*!" exclaimed her husband. "It was a quick ending to his chapter of life—there must be many worse deaths than that."

Suddenly Dorothy sat up and, taking Marani's hand, looked into her dark eyes.

"When did he die?" she asked softly.

"Three days ago, *mem*."

Bently uttered an inarticulate sound, and his wife clutched at the nearest chair for I support.

"Come back and see me to-morrow," she whispered to the girl, and Marani disappeared in the darkness.

Arthur Bently crossed the verandah and took her into his strong arms.

At breakfast the following morning the manager of Limana looked across the table at Mrs. Bently.

"Let me see," he said, "how long have you two been married now?"

"Nearly three months," said Dorothy, and stooped down behind the table to pick up her fallen serviette.

VIII. THE VENGEANCE OF LI-HIP-SEE

THE TROPIC SUN BEAT DOWN upon the rubber-grown slopes of the Limana Kabun, upon the scores of sweating, half-naked coolies toiling between the trees, and upon the distant sweep of very blue sea just visible from Dane's verandah.

It was mid-afternoon, and a plague of tiny sand-flies heightened the discomfort of the great heat. Under the house hens busily scratched in the soil, and two terriers lay peacefully sleeping, one eye always half open for any chance trespassers on the path which wound up the hill past the front of the manager's house.

Behind the manager's bungalow there was nothing but rubber for a couple of miles or more, and all around spoke of prosperity and good management. Dane, who had succeeded Hansard, had indeed justified his promotion. Old. ramshackle buildings had been scrapped wholesale, and new, well-built stores, hospital, and coolie lines had sprung up in their place. A director had lately paid a surprise visit to the estate, and it was now a certainty that if by any chance Hansard should return from the wilds, where he was believed to have perished, he would be paid off in favour of Dane. The director had heard too many rumours about the ex-manager's habits.

Dorothy Bently dropped the novel she had been reading and called across the broad verandah to her husband, who was busily checking a fat typewritten report relating to the trade of the past year.

"Arthur!"

"Hullo!" He threw his cigar-end over the rail and looked up from his work.

"Are you very busy?"

Bently smiled and turned the report over face downwards on the deal table.

"Never too busy to talk to you, dear. What is it?"

He drew a long cane chair next to hers and gently relieved her of her book.

"That's better. Now we can talk comfortably. Phew! It's pretty hot this afternoon, and these flies are the very deuce! Well, dear?"

"Nearly a week ago, Arthur, we learnt of George's death from the lips of the Dusun girl, Marani. There was no doubt that my late husband was the man she had met, for the locket she brought me was the one he had always worn, and I feel sure, Arthur, that, however bad he may have been, his regard for me was such that he would never have given that to a living soul—even if he were starving."

Arthur Bently pressed her hand, but said nothing. He seemed to understand her so much better than her first husband had done.

"I may be very foolish," she continued, "to still worry about things as I do, but somehow I can't get it off my mind—however much I try. I know now he is dead, and yet—and yet I don't quite know how to explain it, but he haunts me."

"Haunts you!" Bently sat bolt upright in his chair and stared at his wife in amazement. "Haunts you! What do you mean?"

"Oh, it isn't easy to believe or understand. It isn't strange forms I see when I'm alone, I don't hear voices in the air or wake to find his ghostly form bending over me. There is nothing like that in my case. It's just this, I can't get him off my mind. I wonder, Arthur, if there is really anything in the old superstition—"

"What superstition, dear?"

"Why, that when a body is unburied the spirit which once inhabited it cannot rest until the remains are covered."

Bently whistled and beat a tattoo with his finger-tips on the arm of his long chair.

"It's a theory that *does* play an important part in fiction," he said, "but—well, you know, I'm one of those practical sort of fellows who's never encountered a ghost; I rather doubt if I should recognize one if I saw it."

He leaned a little down towards her. "Do you really mean it?" he asked softly. "Do you wish me to go and find him and give him a decent burial? Because I will, you know, to-morrow—if you ask me. For all his faults, and for all he did to ruin me in the early days, he was once one of the best pals a man could wish for—my only chum, in fact. It was drink that proved his ruin—alcohol plays the very devil with a man anywhere, but out here—it's awful! I wanted to kill him once, you know, but you unwittingly prevented me. Dorothy, we both loved him once, and it was his one great vice that came be-

tween us in both cases. Let us think of him as one of
Fate's fools—a victim of circumstance and envi-
ronment."

She threw both her arms around his sunburnt neck
and kissed him many times.

"I will start to-morrow at dawn," he said. "I know
you want me to go, and I should like to do the only
thing I can for him now. Boy!"

A pig-tailed head appeared round the corner of the
door. "Yah, *tuan*?"

"Find me Marani—the Dusun girl who lives at the
hut of Li-Hip-See—No. 3 Konzsie. Send her to me
at once. *Tahu?*"

The head disappeared, and soon afterwards a pattering of bare feet was heard from the pathway at the
back of the house. Ten minutes later Marani stood
before them, looking very young and very maidenly
in her black velvet coat with huge silver brooches to
fasten it and her shining sarong of a brilliant green.
Her shining black hair was neatly drawn back and
rolled into a long, cylindrical mass at the back in
true Borneo .fashion, and the neat gold ear-rings and
studs of the same metal in her nose called attention
to the fine formation of her features.

"The white *tuan* would speak to me," she said
simply. "I am here to listen and obey."

"To-morrow before sunrise I must be away to the
place where you saw the *Tuan* Hansard fall, and I
shall want you to go with me to act as guide. For this
I will give you fifty dollars."

Marani looked at her toes and fidgeted with them
on the bare floor of the verandah.

"The white *tuan* is kind," she whispered, "but the way is long and the river is unsafe to those who know it not. One must think many times before venturing so far. There are crocodiles and many snakes and great orang-outangs in the trees."

Bently knitted his brows and gazed at her sternly.

"To-morrow we go," he said shortly, "and you must accompany me. Tahu?"

The girl nodded and was about to retire down the steps, when Dane, the manager, came in, threw his topi on to the table, and sat heavily down in the nearest chair, mopping his brow with a large red handkerchief.

"Phew, it's sweltering!" he said, "and deuced thirsty walking!"

"Look here, Dane," said Bently in English, so that Marani might not understand. "That girl is to take me to-morrow to where Hansard died. I want to give him a decent burial. She seems rather reluctant, although I've offered her fifty dollars for the job. She's got to accompany me, and so I'd like you to instruct your watchman to keep an eye on her to-night in case she vanishes as mysteriously as she appeared."

"Certainly, old man." He shouted for the boy and cooling drinks. "You'll go up the river in your steam-launch, I suppose? She's a handy little craft, and I'll lend you a watchman with a rifle in case of trouble. You've got your Malay mechanic and your boy—with the black girl you'll find the boat pretty full up as it is. From her descriptions of the place, barring accident, you should be there in about a day."

A tall Pathan watchman in gorgeous uniform of khaki and red appeared in front of the verandah.

"See that you never lose sight of the black girl," Dane whispered, leaning over the verandah. "To-morrow you accompany the *Tuan* Bently on an ex-pedition. You must make certain all food necessary for three days is placed on board his launch, and take your rifle and plenty of ammunition."

The watchman saluted and stepped back a few paces to allow Marani to pass on her way back to the hut of Li-Hip-See.

"It is well," said the crippled Chinese cook when Marani had told him of the proposed journey. "I have hated him for what he did to me for so long a time that I should like to see him dead before I could really believe he was no more."

"Then you would come, too?" Marani's eyes glowed like two live coals. If by any chance the poi-soned dart had failed to do its work thoroughly, she had in Li-Hip-See a valuable accomplice—one who nursed an ever-smouldering hate for a terrible wrong done to him by their mutual enemy.

"Very well," she whispered presently, "I will see the *Tuan* Bently and ask him to take you instead of his own boy—who is not very well, I know. Tell me"—she leered forward, until her face almost touched his—"if he is not dead, what will you do?"

Li-Hip-See slipped a claw-like hand into his long coat and drew out a wicked-looking blade, more than a foot in length, but very sharp and thin.

"With this I could carve the very heart out of a man!" he hissed, and Marani, smiling, began weav-ing a basket she had started making two days before.

"But he *is* dead," she whispered, after a long while, "because I puffed a poisoned arrow at him, swiftly and surely, and saw him crash heavily to the ground—so."

She hammered with her fist on the wooden door.

George Hansard was not dead! When Marani's cry of victory had died away and her canoe had long vanished round the bend of the stream, the planter staggered to his feet and plucked the tiny dart from his arm. He felt dizzy and faint, and perspiration oozed from every pore. He had a dim notion that he ought to have died when the poison entered his flesh. He steadied himself and, bending down, dipped the wounded arm in the cooling waters of the river. Then he lanced the wound with the razor-like blade of the *kris* he had taken from the black girl, and let the blood run for a while before tearing a strip from his singlet and binding the place as best he could.

"Ah," he muttered after a while, "that's better. I can see things pretty clearly again. I wonder if the little devil will come back to make sure? She'll find a pretty warm welcome waiting for her when she does. Lord! I'm as thirsty as a damn fish!"

He stooped and picked up the dart. He turned it over carefully in his hand and then tossed it into the stream.

"The arrows were damped through lying too long in the canoe," he decided. "Perhaps they were splashed when Dahamin killed Mellor. The poison must have washed off or been considerably weakened. It must have been an exciting finish, that fight—the white against the black, at night, in those damnably frail canoes. I'm glad I killed the trader, anyway, when he returned with Mellor's head. Hello!"

He peered through the bushes at something he had noticed, and then plunged headlong in the direction of a low native hut he had never seen before. It was raised only a couple of feet above the ground, and the door was fastened by a weak wooden catch. He pulled it open and looked in. Then he laughed aloud and stepped on to the raised wooden floor.

There were bales of native cloth strewn around, a pile of Dusun weapons in one corner—*parang*s, spears, and a straight, double-bladed *kris*—three or four battered lanterns, a barrel of oil, gourds, cooking utensils, and baskets of cheap finery. He had discovered the dead trader's secret store. One thing caught his eye and made his throat feel dry and his palate yearn for the taste of liquor. There were at least a dozen large earthenware bottles of the liquor he had lately learned to love—*samsu*. Here, near at hand, was a supply of drink, food, weapons, and clothing to last him for many days to come. He slipped one of the bottles under his arm and closed the door carefully.

He had read somewhere that whisky was good for snake-bite; perhaps *samsu*, a native liquor, was an effective antidote for a dose of *sumpitan* poisoning. He found his way back by the river to the little hut in the clearing.

It would be very lonely here now, he knew; no one to talk to, no one to cook for him, no one to alleviate the monotony of his exile. He removed the wax which sealed the cork into the jar, and threw the cork into the clearing. Crouching on the native mat by the little doorway, he poured some of the strong liquor down his parched throat.

"That was good," he remarked. "It's wonderful what life *samsu* can put into a man when he's seedy. It's a most extraordinary thing, but a few months ago I wouldn't look at the stuff, but now—" He took a second long pull at the bottle and smacked his lips.

"Wonderful!" he ejaculated. "I wonder who invented it?"

The sun had gone down behind the trees and the atmosphere was quickly growing cooler. Insects hummed everywhere, crickets and lizards called shrilly from the sago-leaf walls and roof.

"It's going to be damnably rotten here at night," muttered Hansard, and suddenly darkness fell.

Frightened by the stillness of the vast jungle by day and the voices of its denizens by night, Hansard sought relief in copious draughts of *samsu*. With a store of the liquor always to hand, his self-control vanished, and two days after Marani's departure the old failing had gripped him, and he rolled wildly about the clearing and the floor of the little hut, drunk—always drunk! As soon as the effect of one night of dissipation had partly worn off, he thirsted for something to ease it, and he sought relief in the dread *samsu*—that compound of *arak* that had twice before proved his ruin. His beard had grown long, and his matted hair ran riot over his ears, face, and neck. His skin was growing dark with constant exposure to the glare of the tropical sun, and he had at last discarded the only garment that acted as a kind of link between himself and his kind—his tattered khaki jacket. He had worn that coat—day in, day out—ever since that day, months ago, when he had ridden wildly from his bungalow over the hills and away until the jungle swallowed him. All day and every day, all night and every night, Hansard crouched on the floor of his lonely hut, an earthenware jar at his side, and chewed fibrous tobacco, spitting at intervals into the clearing—just as the lowest native might do. To see him, unkempt and in Dusun costume, squatting at the tiny door or hastening to the secret storehouse in the woods for more liquor, one could never have pictured in him the smart, well-dressed, easy-going young planter's assistant, stepping off the gangway fresh from home, only a matter of seven or eight years before. He never tried to hunt, or to make a canoe or raft in which to find his way down the winding river back to civilization. Drink-sodden and brain-dulled, he was content to drink and sleep—sleep and drink his hours and his health away. What would happen to him when the supply of liquor ran out—as soon it would—he did not trouble to think. Soon, too, the store of food would run low, and he would have to replenish it—or starve.

In his brief intervals of comparative sobriety he never allowed himself to think of the beautiful young wife he had left in the manager's bungalow at the Limana Kabun. He thought sometimes of Marani, the trader's daughter, and sometimes wished he had kept a closer watch on her and prevented her running away with the canoe.

"The world has long assumed that I am dead," he muttered to himself one day, "and now if Marani reaches the coast she will tell them, perhaps, that she has seen me die. Well, what of it? I *am* dead. I shall never go back. One day a great beast of the jungle will find me in the clearing and tear me, or I shall fall into the river and the crocs will make a meal of me."

He shuddered and reached for the earthenware jar of liquor to drown the unpleasant reflections of his disordered brain.

That night he awoke from his drunken sleep and, looking from the tiny doorway, saw the spirit of Dahamin—the trader he had killed—standing in the clearing, just at the foot of the rough bamboo ladder. He could see every line of the familiar form, and there was a long hunting-knife protruding from between his shoulder-blades. The vision was so clear that Hansard groaned aloud in terror and buried his head in his hands lest he should go mad with fear. The jungle whispered round him, the palms sighed in the soft night breeze, the *atap*s rustled ceaselessly, and the awfulness of the solitude was intense. He would have given all the contents of his store— his right hand, anything, everything—for the ugliest, darkest man or woman in God's earth to step from the jungle or river-bank into the clearing. But there at the foot of the ladder, in a luminous haze, stood Dahamin—not looking at him reproachfully, but gazing sadly towards the spot where Hansard had surprised and killed him. The planter uttered a wild cry, broke the spell which had momentarily rendered his muscles ineffectual, and, seizing the half-empty bottle of *samsu*, poured the greater part of its contents down his throat.

He thrust a native mat up against the door and wedged it there by means of a wooden case. The darkness within appalled him, and somehow or other he just managed to light the oil-lamp which hung from the roof in the centre of the room. He reeled into a corner, fell heavily on to his mat, and slept—snoring like a pig and muttering to himself all the time. An hour later he knocked his arm on the wall of his hut and woke. He thought he saw the figure of a man he had known years before—a man he had robbed of his share in the Dua-Orang Kabun.

"Good Lord!" he groaned. "Will all the nights after this haunt me? I shall go mad—stark, staring mad! Ah! Get away from me. Get away, Bently! Arthur, for God's sake don't torment me! Oh, my God!"

The form of his old partner seemed to cross the floor and bend over him for a moment—and then was gone. Hansard sat up and wiped the perspiration from his face and neck with his sarong.

"I can't stand much more of this," he murmured. "The *samsu* is losing its effect. It only stupefies me now. It doesn't shut out the present and the future, but it recalls visions of the past, and they frighten me. Lord in heaven, what—what was that?"

He sat bolt upright, his hair almost on end, every nerve strained to discover the nature of a new sound outside—a queer, grating, puffing, snorting sound which seemed a little familiar and yet strange to the wilds. It came from somewhere down towards the river, and it grew louder and louder every minute.

"What is it? What new ghost is coming to haunt me? Is this the hell my sins have brought me to—an existence of perpetual nightmare?"

He listened intently, and then sprang to his feet with a wild cry—

"I hear them! Heavens, what does it mean? Voices and footsteps in the clearing!"

The little puffing steam-launch churned up the waters of the winding river, an armed Pathan at the stern, and Arthur Bently sitting thoughtfully at the bows. Marani stood suddenly at his shoulder. He started and glanced up at her. It was very dark, and the waters of the river rushing swiftly by looked like a sea of dark, swirling oil.

"*Tuan!*"

"Hello! *Apah mahu?*"

"It is near here where he fell—the *Tuan* Hansard."

He shouted an order to the mechanic and the vessel slowed down. Marani shaded her eyes trying to pierce the darkness, and the moon sailed from behind a cloud and shone over the waters of the river, the jungle, and the reeds by its banks.

"It is there, *sana*," she cried hoarsely. "Take the boat in a little way and I will show you."

Li-Hip-See, the crippled Chinese cook, absolutely quivering with excitement, held a lighted hurricane lamp in one hand and stared hard at the spot the girl had indicated. As the vessel drew carefully in all eyes gazed shorewards, trying to detect the remains of the man they were seeking.

The voice of Marani came from the darkness, and it was queer-sounding and strained.

"He is no longer there, *tuan*. His body has gone."

"Perhaps it is not the place. In the darkness the world looks different."

"It is always the same to me, *tuan*, and I tell you he is not there."

"A wild beast has taken him away into the jungle," remarked the Pathan, "or perhaps a crocodile has dragged him into the stream."

The others said nothing, and Li-Hip-See was examining the long sharp blade of his dagger, crooning strangely to himself. "If he has escaped," he muttered, "it were better he had never lived!"

Suddenly Marani cried aloud and clung to Bently in terror.

"*Tuan, tuan*! See, see! There is the hut of which I spoke to you; there is the little clearing, and in the room there is a light."

Bently turned cold all over, and, removing her arms from his coat, ordered the mechanic to run the boat as close in as he could. The body gone—a light in the hut! What in heaven's name did it all mean? He sprang lightly ashore as soon as but a couple of feet separated the boat from the bank and her keel scraped on the soft bed of the river. Marani led the way to the foot of the rickety ladder. They stood in a little group in the clearing—Marani. Bentlv, Li-Hip-See, and the armed Pathan watchman, very erect and fearing nothing.

Arthur Bently turned to the woman.

"Call!" he said. "Call out '*Tuan*!' "

Li-Hip-See started and clutched the arm of the watchman.

"You hear," he hissed. "The *Tuan* Bently thinks that the *Tuan* Hansard is still alive. What else could that call mean?"

"*Tuan*! Tu—an! Tu—an!"

There was a scuffling within, and a rough mat was drawn swiftly away from the opening. Someone was peering out into the darkness. The tall Pathan crept to the wall, and held his lantern so that its rays fell full on the little doorway.

Marani screamed aloud. Li-Hip-See swore fiercely and spat, and Bently, hastening up the ladder, recognized the distorted features of his old friend. "Hansard!"

The man at the doorway started. He passed a weary hand over his brow, and then cried out in a loud voice:

"My God! It's Bently!" and then the lamp flickered and went out.

Arthur Bently turned and came back down the frail ladder which creaked and bent dangerously under his weight. The Pathan was cursing softly to himself in his own tongue, endeavouring to get the lamp to burn satisfactorily. Marani was sobbing, her black head buried in her hands, though why she couldn't quite understand. As the lamp burned up brightly once more, Bently caught sight of the crippled Li-Hip-See leaning on a post which supported the hut sharpening a long, thin blade on the sole of his leathern shoe.

He strode across and shook him roughly by the shoulder.

"What are you doing that for?" he shouted in Malay. "There's no danger now, you damned idiot!"

He would have snatched the weapon away from him, but Li-Hip-See was a little too quick for him and his hand was already underneath his thin blue coat.

"I am hungry, *tuan*, that is all, and a knife is best when it is sharp."

Bently shrugged his shoulders. "Come on, now," he bellowed. "Back to the boat every one of you, and keep her in readiness to start in half an hour. Watchman No. 4, just keep a sharp eye on that black girl; she's too near home to be allowed to stray."

The little group by the hut broke up in obedience to Bently's commands. Marani stood for a moment in the centre of the clearing, thinking. Hansard would tell Bently she had tried to murder him, and she had some vague notion that the white men have dire penalties for such offences. What should she do? Li-Hip-See! She must approach him and solicit his assistance. Hansard must be got out of the way somehow, unless—unless she managed to escape while the two white men talked.

A heavy hand fell upon her shoulder.

"Come along; no dawdling here, you *hoonoon*! There's plenty of room for thinking on board."

She turned in sudden fury on the stalwart Pathan watchman, who, without a moment's hesitation, seized her in his powerful arms and bore her, struggling and biting, to the waiting steam-launch, which put out into midstream immediately afterwards. She looked over the side as he dropped her on to her feet.

"*Jaga-jaga!* (be careful!)," he said, "the crocodiles are hungry to-night." He put both hands on his hips and laughed. Marani, shaking with fury, turned and spat in his face.

Arthur Bently ascended the bamboo ladder, pushed aside the matting and case which blocked the entrance, and, stooping low so as to avoid knocking his head, stepped inside the hut and closed the entrance in the same manner after him. Hansard was crouching in one corner, his head in his hands, shivering like a man with the ague.

"George!" said Bently softly.

The other man did not look up, but motioned wildly with his hands.

"Go away!" he cried. "For God's sake, leave me alone! I've been hunted enough already! This cursed *samsu* makes me dream!"

Bently crossed the floor, picked up the bottle, and, with all it contained, pitched it through the doorway into the night. Hansard uncovered his eyes and saw what he had done. Quick as thought, his hand sought his *kris*, and he hurled himself like a tiger at his former partner. Bently turned very white, stepped back, tripped him neatly up, and secured the sharp *kris* as it dropped from the drunken man's hand. Hansard sat up on the floor where he had fallen and rubbed his eyes.

"So it is you!" he said thickly. "Where in God's name have you sprung from?"

"I have come to take you back to your wife," said Bently, who was looking at a spider on the opposite wall. He was very calm, but the shock of finding Hansard alive had momentarily dulled his brain, and he dared not try to think of the future.

Hansard staggered suddenly to his feet and faced the other. In the feeble light of the oil-lamp Bently could see how low his old friend had sunk. Drunkenness was written on every feature of his face. His hand shook like an aspen.

"Are you ready!" he asked calmly.

Hansard started. "Ready! Ready! What d'you mean? I'm not going to trust myself to you. You've come here for vengeance. I know you. You remember that business of the Dua-Orang Estate. Why don't you kill me now and here?"

Bently seized his arm and shook him till his teeth chattered.

"Come on, wake up! You're drunk, man!"

Hansard steadied himself, endeavoured to assume an indignant expression, and fell suddenly to the floor with a thud which shook the building. Bently stooped and lifted him up, but he was fast asleep— snoring loudly! He shouted at him, shook him, kicked him, but the drunken man slumbered on. At last, in sheer desperation, he dragged him by the shoulders across the floor and lifted him on to the native mat which served as his bed.

"I'll wait till the morning," he told himself. "He ought to be a trifle more tractable by then. Meantime, I'll go and have a little *makan* on board."

He hurried down the steps and through the clearing. The moon was shining brightly, and he signalled to the watchman to have the boat brought in to shore again. The engine grunted and puffed from mid-stream into shallow water, and Bently leaped on board with agility.

The vessel turned and began steaming out again. Suddenly there came a shock which shook the little craft from stem to stern. The mechanic swore fiercely in Malay, the Pathan watchman narrowly escaped falling overboard, and Bently could see that the vessel had struck a submerged tree trunk. Part of its bottom had been torn away, and the water was fast pouring in.

The Pathan watchman procured a bundle of greasy tow from the mechanic and endeavoured to plug the leak while the boat was being brought into shore. In the confusion, the shock of the collision, the sudden escape of steam, the excited shouting and rushing to and fro, nobody noticed two dark forms plunge into the water and wade shorewards. Marani dragged the bent-up form of Li-Hip-See on to the bank.

"Come quickly," she whispered, "before they notice our absence. Have you still your sharp knife in your belt?"

The Chinaman nodded, and felt for it to make sure he had not lost it in the stream.

"Good! Then come with me quietly—so—through here. Are you following?" She looked back over her shoulder.

They stood together in the moonlit clearing, Marani very erect and very calm, Li-Hip-See bent nearly double and quivering with excitement and emotion. It became dark again, and a chill wind rustled the sago-leaf roof above. A startled bird shrieked in a palm-tree, and from the river came the sound of curses as Bently and his man maneuvered the wrecked launch.

"Quick!" she hissed. "Remember how he trampled you under foot. Remember the good white *mem* who was his wife, and is now married to another. Remember all things and strike swiftly and surely."

Li-Hip-See, not uttering a word, scrambled up the ladder and through the opening above. Marani waited below, her heart beating wildly, straining her ears to catch any sound from within.

Arthur Bently sat on the river's bank smoking his blackened briar. In the morning he would bring Hansard back to his wife. Hansard had scored after all, and, although Bently knew little of the law in such matters, he was well aware that Dorothy and he were guilty of bigamy.

"It's deucedly unkind of Fate to have drawn me here to-night," he said; "and a man like that who's got so low might just as well have died instead of returning to life to ruin the happiness of others."

He rose and paced up and down the bank.

"To-morrow—to-morrow—to-morrow!"   The words hammered in his brain. Would to heaven the morrow might never come!

He started and turned. Full in the moonlight, twenty yards away, stood Marani, looking very fine and very beautiful. In her hand she poised something large and round.

"*Tuan*," she cried softly, "I have a present here for you. It is worthless—quite—and yet it means everything to you. *Tabi, tuan, tabi!*"

She rolled the object towards him and disappeared into the jungle as swiftly and silently as a wild cat stalks a bird.

He laughed, advanced a few paces, and stooped down. A sudden horror seized him—a certain vague suspicion her words had slowly evolved in his brain.

He felt in a side pocket, found an oblong box, and nervously drew out a match. His hands shook so that he had to strike at least half a dozen before he could get a light. He knelt on the ground, held the match low, and looked—then he uttered a wild, inarticulate cry and sprang to his feet.

"Watchman! *Lakas!* Search the woods. Find that woman at all costs, and that crippled Chinaman with the knife."

He tore madly through the woods, almost beside himself, while on the ground by the river's bank lay the severed head of George Hansard!

EDMUND SNELL: SOME NOTES TOWARD A BIBLIOGRAPHY

To preface this, I must apologize for the woeful incompleteness of the document that follows. Edmund Snell was a remarkably prolific author, but very little has been done in terms of presenting a bibliography of his work. This is starting point, that's all, just a starting point. His books are fairly well documented, as is his work that appeared in the story paper, *The Thriller* (thanks to the work of Steve Holland), but this barely scratches the surface. Snell wrote dozens, rather hundreds of stories in all genres and throughout the 1920s and 1930s it was pretty near impossible to pick up a British fiction magazine and *not* find a Snell story.

We will certainly add information as it becomes available, for now we know of the following (*to be published by Ramble House):

*The Yellow Seven (London: T. Fisher Unwin 1923)
*Corrigan's Way (London: T. Fisher Unwin 1924)
*The Crimson Butterfly (London: T. Fisher Unwin 1924)

*The Yu-Chi Stone
(London: T. Fisher Unwin 1925)

*Blue Murder (London: T. Fisher
Unwin 1927)

*The Purple Shadow (London: T.
Fisher Unwin 1927)

Kontrol (London: Ernest Benn,
1928) (Philadelphia: J. B. Lip-
pincott, 1928)

*The White Owl (London: Hodder & Stoughton
1930)

*The Sound Machine (London:
Skeffington & Son 1932)

*The Z Ray (London: Skeffington
& Son 1932)

*And Then...One Dark Night
(London: Skeffington & Son
1933)

Crooks Ltd. (London: Skeffington
& Son 1934)

*The Sign of the Scorpion (London:
Skeffington & Son 1935)

*Murder at the Miramar (London:
Skeffington & Son 1936)

*Yellow Jacket: The Return of
Chanda-Lung (London: Skeffington & Son 1936)

*The Back of Beyond (London:
Philip Allan 1936) (Note: This is
a novel, not a collection!)

Grid Murder (London: Mellifont Press 1937)

*The Red Spinner (London: Robert Hale & Co.
1937)

*The Crimson Swastika (London: Mellifont Press 1938)

*The Finger of Destiny (London: Quality Press 1938) (Expanded edition from Dancing Tuatara Press)

*Murder in Switzerland (London: Robert Hale & Co. 1938)

Anti-Crime Ltd (London: Mellifont Press 1939)

Calling All Cars (London: Mellifont Press 1939)

Back from the Dead (London: Mellifont Press 1940)

Suicide House (London: Mellifont Press 1941)

*The Dope Dealer (London: Mellifont Press 1941)

Emerald of Death (London: Everybody's 1944)

Research indicates that the "books" published by Mellifont were in fact, chapbooks, often less than 60 pages in length. It is likely that this material will be incorporated into new collections, (of which we already have four in the early stages of preparation.)

EDMUND SNELL IN *THE THRILLER*

NOTE: Most of these pieces are of novella length and will be collected in volumes comprised of three or four selections and released from either Dancing Tuatara Press or Ramble House based on content. The more outré or weird pieces will be issued by DTP; the more straight-forward crime stories will be from RH. It is our intent to republish as much of this material as possible.

Alias the Stoat 7/16/32
The Black Dagger 8/15/31
The Case of the Captured Spy 8/24/35
Crook versus Crook 4/8/33
The Curse of Osaris 7/18/36
The Curse of the Phari 1/4/30
The Death Mask 2/15/30
The Death Roll 11/8/30
The Death Ship 2/5/33
The Death Sign 7/26/30
The Diamond Gang 5/23/31
The Double Diamond 11/23/29
The Fatal Quest 12/17/32
The Five Aces 5/3/30
The Frozen Hawk 1/20/34
Gang Bait 4/4/31
The Gas Gang 12/13/30

The Great Hiking Mystery 9/12/31

The Green Feather 6/29/29

Grey Mask 9/2/33

The Hold-up Gang 2/28/31

The Hounds of Hoffman 7/8/39

The House of Fear 5/18/29

The Man from Moscow 1/24/31

The Man in Black 9/24/32

The Man in the Wheeled Chair 5/9/36

The Mystery of Blackstone Manor 10/29/32

The Night of Terror 11/28/31

The Non-stop Gang 10/10/31

Racket Rule 7/11/31

The Red Racketeer 7/8/33

The Secret of the Discs 8/29/36

The Seven Shadows 7/11/32

The Seventh Door 6/14/30

The Sign of the Red Arab 9/29/34

Sinister Ship 4/2/32

Smith of the Legion 7/7/34

The Smugglers Victim 11/4/33

The Talking Skull 1/21/33

The Telephone Box Mystery 5/16/36

Tong Law 5/29/30

Trail of Death 8/27/32
The Vendetta 9/27/30
The Web of Wu Kang 10/24/36
White Mask 10/5/29
The White Snake 8/18/34
The Yellow Death 2/20/32

And in *Top Notch* the novel *Green Jade Magic* was serialized from October 15, 1925 through January 1, 1926. We do hope to someday be able to reprint this novel.

RAMBLE HOUSE's

HARRY STEPHEN KEELER WEBWORK MYSTERIES

(RH) indicates the title is available ONLY in the RAMBLE HOUSE edition

The Ace of Spades Murder
The Affair of the Bottled Deuce (RH)
The Amazing Web
The Barking Clock
Behind That Mask
The Book with the Orange Leaves
The Bottle with the Green Wax Seal
The Box from Japan
The Case of the Canny Killer
The Case of the Crazy Corpse (RH)
The Case of the Flying Hands (RH)
The Case of the Ivory Arrow
The Case of the Jeweled Ragpicker
The Case of the Lavender Gripsack
The Case of the Mysterious Moll
The Case of the 16 Beans
The Case of the Transparent Nude (RH)
The Case of the Transposed Legs
The Case of the Two-Headed Idiot (RH)
The Case of the Two Strange Ladies
The Circus Stealers (RH)
Cleopatra's Tears
A Copy of Beowulf (RH)
The Crimson Cube (RH)
The Face of the Man From Saturn
Find the Clock
The Five Silver Buddhas
The 4th King
The Gallows Waits, My Lord! (RH)
The Green Jade Hand
Finger! Finger!
Hangman's Nights (RH)
I, Chameleon (RH)
I Killed Lincoln at 10:13! (RH)
The Iron Ring
The Man Who Changed His Skin (RH)
The Man with the Crimson Box
The Man with the Magic Eardrums
The Man with the Wooden Spectacles
The Marceau Case
The Matilda Hunter Murder

The Monocled Monster
The Murder of London Lew
The Murdered Mathematician
The Mysterious Card (RH)
The Mysterious Ivory Ball of Wong Shing Li (RH)
The Mystery of the Fiddling Cracksman
The Peacock Fan
The Photo of Lady X (RH)
The Portrait of Jirjohn Cobb
Report on Vanessa Hewstone (RH)
Riddle of the Travelling Skull
Riddle of the Wooden Parrakeet (RH)
The Scarlet Mummy (RH)
The Search for X-Y-Z
The Sharkskin Book
Sing Sing Nights
The Six From Nowhere (RH)
The Skull of the Waltzing Clown
The Spectacles of Mr. Cagliostro
Stand By—London Calling!
The Steeltown Strangler
The Stolen Gravestone (RH)
Strange Journey (RH)
The Strange Will
The Straw Hat Murders (RH)
The Street of 1000 Eyes (RH)
Thieves' Nights
Three Novellos (RH)
The Tiger Snake
The Trap (RH)
Vagabond Nights (Defrauded Yeggman)
Vagabond Nights 2 (10 Hours)
The Vanishing Gold Truck
The Voice of the Seven Sparrows
The Washington Square Enigma
When Thief Meets Thief
The White Circle (RH)
The Wonderful Scheme of Mr. Christo-
    pher Thorne
X. Jones—of Scotland Yard
Y. Cheung, Business Detective

Keeler Related Works

A To Izzard: A Harry Stephen Keeler Companion by Fender Tucker — Articles and stories about Harry, by Harry, and in his style. Included is a compleat bibliography.

Wild About Harry: Reviews of Keeler Novels — Edited by Richard Polt & Fender Tucker — 22 reviews of works by Harry Stephen Keeler from *Keeler News*. A perfect introduction to the author.

The Keeler Keyhole Collection: Annotated newsletter rants from Harry Stephen Keeler, edited by Francis M. Nevins. Over 400 pages of incredibly personal Keeleriana.

Fakealoo — Pastiches of the style of Harry Stephen Keeler by selected demented members of the HSK Society. Updated every year with the new winner.

Strands of the Web: Short Stories of Harry Stephen Keeler — 29 stories, just about all that Keeler wrote, are edited and introduced by Fred Cleaver.

RAMBLE HOUSE's LOON SANCTUARY

A Clear Path to Cross — Sharon Knowles short mystery stories by Ed Lynskey.

A Corpse Walks in Brooklyn and Other Stories — Volume 5 in the Day Keene in the Detective Pulps series.

A Jimmy Starr Omnibus — Three 40s novels by Jimmy Starr.

A Niche in Time and Other Stories — Classic SF by William F. Temple

A Roland Daniel Double: The Signal and The Return of Wu Fang — Classic thrillers from the 30s.

A Shot Rang Out — Three decades of reviews and articles by today's Anthony Boucher, Jon Breen. An essential book for any mystery lover's library.

A Smell of Smoke — A 1951 English countryside thriller by Miles Burton.

A Snark Selection — Lewis Carroll's *The Hunting of the Snark* with two Snarkian chapters by Harry Stephen Keeler — Illustrated by Gavin L. O'Keefe.

A Young Man's Heart — A forgotten early classic by Cornell Woolrich.

Alexander Laing Novels — *The Motives of Nicholas Holtz* and *Dr. Scarlett*, stories of medical mayhem and intrigue from the 30s.

An Angel in the Street — Modern hardboiled noir by Peter Genovese.

Automaton — Brilliant treatise on robotics: 1928-style! By H. Stafford Hatfield.

Away From the Here and Now — Clare Winger Harris stories, collected by Richard A. Lupoff

Beast or Man? — A 1930 novel of racism and horror by Sean M'Guire. Introduced by John Pelan.

Black Beadle — A 1939 thriller by E.C.R. Lorac.

Black Hogan Strikes Again — Australia's Peter Renwick pens a tale of the 30s outback.

Black River Falls — Suspense from the master, Ed Gorman.

Blondy's Boy Friend — A snappy 1930 story by Philip Wylie, writing as Leatrice Homesley.

Blood in a Snap — The *Finnegan's Wake* of the 21st century, by Jim Weiler.

Blood Moon — The first of the Robert Payne series by Ed Gorman.

Bogart '48 — Hollywood action with Bogie by John Stanley and Kenn Davis.

Calling Lou Largo! — Two Lou Largo novels by William Ard.

Cornucopia of Crime — Francis M. Nevins assembled this huge collection of his writings about crime literature and the people who write it. Essential for any serious mystery library.

Corpse Without Flesh — Strange novel of forensics by George Bruce

Crimson Clown Novels — By Johnston McCulley, author of the Zorro novels, *The Crimson Clown* and *The Crimson Clown Again*.

Dago Red — 22 tales of dark suspense by Bill Pronzini.

Dark Sanctuary — Weird Menace story by H. B. Gregory.

David Hume Novels — *Corpses Never Argue, Cemetery First Stop, Make Way for the Mourners, Eternity Here I Come*. 1930s British hardboiled fiction with an attitude.

Dead Man Talks Too Much — Hollywood boozer by Weed Dickenson.

Death Leaves No Card — One of the most unusual murdered-in-the-tub mysteries you'll ever read. By Miles Burton.

Death March of the Dancing Dolls and Other Stories — Volume Three in the Day Keene in the Detective Pulps series. Introduced by Bill Crider.

Deep Space and other Stories — A collection of SF gems by Richard A. Lupoff.

Detective Duff Unravels It — Episodic mysteries by Harvey O'Higgins.

Diabolic Candelabra — Classic 30s mystery by E.R. Punshon

Dictator's Way — Another D.S. Bobby Owen mystery from E.R. Punshon

Dime Novels: Ramble House's 10-Cent Books — *Knife in the Dark* by Robert Leslie Bellem, *Hot Lead* and *Song of Death* by Ed Earl Repp, *A Hashish House in New York* by H.H. Kane, and five more.

Doctor Arnoldi — Tiffany Thayer's story of the death of death.

Don Diablo: Book of a Lost Film — Two-volume treatment of a western by Paul Landres, with diagrams. Intro by Francis M. Nevins.

Dope and Swastikas — Two strange novels from 1922 by Edmund Snell

Dope Tales #1 — Two dope-riddled classics; *Dope Runners* by Gerald Grantham and *Death Takes the Joystick* by Phillip Condé.

Mark of the Laughing Death and Other Stories — Shockers from the pulps by Francis James, introduced by John Pelan.

Master of Souls — Mark Hansom's 1937 shocker is introduced by weirdologist John Pelan.

Max Afford Novels — *Owl of Darkness, Death's Mannikins, Blood on His Hands, The Dead Are Blind, The Sheep and the Wolves, Sinners in Paradise* and *Two Locked Room Mysteries and a Ripping Yarn* by one of Australia's finest mystery novelists.

Money Brawl — Two books about the writing business by Jack Woodford and H. Bedford-Jones. Introduced by Richard A. Lupoff.

More Secret Adventures of Sherlock Holmes — Gary Lovisi's second collection of tales about the unknown sides of the great detective.

Muddled Mind: Complete Works of Ed Wood, Jr. — David Hayes and Hayden Davis deconstruct the life and works of the mad, but canny, genius.

Murder among the Nudists — A mystery from 1934 by Peter Hunt, featuring a naked Detective-Inspector going undercover in a nudist colony.

Murder in Black and White — 1931 classic tennis whodunit by Evelyn Elder.

Murder in Shawnee — Two novels of the Alleghenies by John Douglas: *Shawnee Alley Fire* and *Haunts*.

Murder in Silk — A 1937 Yellow Peril novel of the silk trade by Ralph Trevor.

My Deadly Angel — 1955 Cold War drama by John Chelton.

My First Time: The One Experience You Never Forget — Michael Birchwood — 64 true first-person narratives of how they lost it.

Mysterious Martin, the Master of Murder — Two versions of a strange 1912 novel by Tod Robbins about a man who writes books that can kill.

Norman Berrow Novels — *The Bishop's Sword, Ghost House, Don't Go Out After Dark, Claws of the Cougar, The Smokers of Hashish, The Secret Dancer, Don't Jump Mr. Boland!, The Footprints of Satan, Fingers for Ransom, The Three Tiers of Fantasy, The Spaniard's Thumb, The Eleventh Plague, Words Have Wings, One Thrilling Night, The Lady's in Danger, It Howls at Night, The Terror in the Fog, Oil Under the Window, Murder in the Melody, The Singing Room.* This is the complete Norman Berrow library of locked-room mysteries, several of which are masterpieces.

Old Faithful and Other Stories — SF classic tales by Raymond Z. Gallun

Old Times' Sake — Short stories by James Reasoner from Mike Shayne Magazine.

One Dreadful Night — A classic mystery by Ronald S. L. Harding

Pair O' Jacks — A mystery novel and a diatribe about publishing by Jack Woodford

Perfect .38 — Two early Timothy Dane novels by William Ard. More to come.

Prince Pax — Devilish intrigue by George Sylvester Viereck and Philip Eldridge

Prose Bowl — Futuristic satire of a world where hack writing has replaced football as our national obsession, by Bill Pronzini and Barry N. Malzberg.

Red Light — The history of legal prostitution in Shreveport Louisiana by Eric Brock. Includes wonderful photos of the houses and the ladies.

Researching American-Made Toy Soldiers — A 276-page collection of a lifetime of articles by toy soldier expert Richard O'Brien.

Reunion in Hell — Volume One of the John H. Knox series of weird stories from the pulps. Introduced by horror expert John Pelan.

Ripped from the Headlines! — The Jack the Ripper story as told in the newspaper articles in the *New York* and *London Times*.

Rough Cut & New, Improved Murder — Ed Gorman's first two novels.

R.R. Ryan Novels — Freak Museum and The Subjugated Beast, two horror classics.

Ruby of a Thousand Dreams — The villain Wu Fang returns in this Roland Daniel novel.

Ruled By Radio — 1925 futuristic novel by Robert L. Hadfield & Frank E. Farncombe.

Rupert Penny Novels — *Policeman's Holiday, Policeman's Evidence, Lucky Policeman, Policeman in Armour, Sealed Room Murder, Sweet Poison, The Talkative Policeman, She had to Have Gas* and *Cut and Run* (by Martin Tanner.) Rupert Penny is the pseudonym of Australian Charles Thornett, a master of the locked room, impossible crime plot.

Sacred Locomotive Flies — Richard A. Lupoff's psychedelic SF story.

Sam — Early gay novel by Lonnie Coleman.

Sand's Game — Spectacular hard-boiled noir from Ennis Willie, edited by Lynn Myers and Stephen Mertz, with contributions from Max Allan Collins, Bill Crider, Wayne

Dundee, Bill Pronzini, Gary Lovisi and James Reasoner.

Sand's War — More violent fiction from the typewriter of Ennis Willie

Satan's Den Exposed — True crime in Truth or Consequences New Mexico — Award-winning journalism by the *Desert Journal.*

Satans of Saturn — Novellas from the pulps by Otis Adelbert Kline and E. H. Price

Satan's Sin House and Other Stories — Horrific gore by Wayne Rogers

Secrets of a Teenage Superhero — Graphic lit by Jonathan Sweet

Sex Slave — Potboiler of lust in the days of Cleopatra by Dion Leclerq, 1966.

Sideslip — 1968 SF masterpiece by Ted White and Dave Van Arnam.

Slammer Days — Two full-length prison memoirs: *Men into Beasts* (1952) by George Sylvester Viereck and *Home Away From Home* (1962) by Jack Woodford.

Slippery Staircase — 1930s whodunit from E.C.R. Lorac

Sorcerer's Chessmen — John Pelan introduces this 1939 classic by Mark Hansom.

Star Griffin — Michael Kurland's 1987 masterpiece of SF drollery is back.

Stakeout on Millennium Drive — Award-winning Indianapolis Noir by Ian Woollen.

Strands of the Web: Short Stories of Harry Stephen Keeler — Edited and Introduced by Fred Cleaver.

Summer Camp for Corpses and Other Stories — Weird Menace tales from Arthur Leo Zagat; introduced by John Pelan.

Suzy — A collection of comic strips by Richard O'Brien and Bob Vojtko from 1970.

Tales of the Macabre and Ordinary — Modern twisted horror by Chris Mikul, author of the *Bizarrism* series.

Tales of Terror and Torment #1 — John Pelan selects and introduces this sampler of weird menace tales from the pulps.

Tenebrae — Ernest G. Henham's 1898 horror tale brought back.

The Amorous Intrigues & Adventures of Aaron Burr — by Anonymous. Hot historical action about the man who almost became Emperor of Mexico.

The Anthony Boucher Chronicles — edited by Francis M. Nevins. Book reviews by Anthony Boucher written for the *San Francisco Chronicle,* 1942 – 1947. Essential and fascinating reading by the best book reviewer there ever was.

The Barclay Catalogs — Two essential books about toy soldier collecting by Richard O'Brien

The Basil Wells Omnibus — A collection of Wells' stories by Richard A. Lupoff

The Beautiful Dead and Other Stories — Dreadful tales from Donald Dale

The Best of 10-Story Book — edited by Chris Mikul, over 35 stories from the literary magazine Harry Stephen Keeler edited.

The Black Dark Murders — Vintage 50s college murder yarn by Milt Ozaki, writing as Robert O. Saber.

The Book of Time — The classic novel by H.G. Wells is joined by sequels by Wells himself and three stories by Richard A. Lupoff. Illustrated by Gavin L. O'Keefe.

The Case in the Clinic — One of E.C.R. Lorac's finest.

The Strange Case of the Antlered Man — A mystery of superstition by Edwy Searles Brooks.

The Case of the Bearded Bride — #4 in the Day Keene in the Detective Pulps series

The Case of the Little Green Men — Mack Reynolds wrote this love song to sci-fi fans back in 1951 and it's now back in print.

The Case of the Withered Hand — 1936 potboiler by John G. Brandon.

The Charlie Chaplin Murder Mystery — A 2004 tribute by noted film scholar, Wes D. Gehring.

The Chinese Jar Mystery — Murder in the manor by John Stephen Strange, 1934.

The Cloudbuilders and Other Stories — SF tales from Colin Kapp.

The Compleat Calhoon — All of Fender Tucker's works: Includes *Totah Six-Pack, Weed, Women and Song* and *Tales from the Tower,* plus a CD of all of his songs.

The Compleat Ova Hamlet — Parodies of SF authors by Richard A. Lupoff. This is a brand new edition with more stories and more illustrations by Trina Robbins.

The Contested Earth and Other SF Stories — A never-before published space opera and seven short stories by Jim Harmon.

The Crimson Query — A 1929 thriller from Arlton Eadie. A perfect way to get introduced.

The Curse of Cantire — Classic 1939 novel of a family curse by Walter S. Masterman.

The Devil and the C.I.D. — Odd diabolic mystery by E.C.R. Lorac

The Devil Drives — An odd prison and lost treasure novel from 1932 by Virgil Markham.

The Devil of Pei-Ling — Herbert Asbury's 1929 tale of the occult.

The Devil's Mistress — A 1915 Scottish gothic tale by J. W. Brodie-Innes, a member of Aleister Crowley's Golden Dawn.

The Devil's Nightclub and Other Stories — John Pelan introduces some gruesome tales by Nat Schachner.

The Disentanglers — Episodic intrigue at the turn of last century by Andrew Lang

The Dog Poker Code — A spoof of *The Da Vinci Code* by D.B. Smithee.

The Dumpling — Political murder from 1907 by Coulson Kernahan.

The End of It All and Other Stories — Ed Gorman selected his favorite short stories for this huge collection.

The Fangs of Suet Pudding — A 1944 novel of the German invasion by Adams Farr

The Finger of Destiny and Other Stories — Edmund Snell's superb collection of weird stories of Borneo.

The Ghost of Gaston Revere — From 1935, a novel of life and beyond by Mark Hansom, introduced by John Pelan.

The Girl in the Dark — A thriller from Roland Daniel

The Gold Star Line — Seaboard adventure from L.T. Reade and Robert Eustace.

The Golden Dagger — 1951 Scotland Yard yarn by E. R. Punshon.

The Great Orme Terror — Horror stories by Garnett Radcliffe from the pulps

The Hairbreadth Escapes of Major Mendax — Francis Blake Crofton's 1889 boys' book.

The House That Time Forgot and Other Stories — Insane pulpitude by Robert F. Young

The House of the Vampire — 1907 poetic thriller by George S. Viereck.

The Illustrious Corpse — Murder hijinx from Tiffany Thayer

The Incredible Adventures of Rowland Hern — Intriguing 1928 impossible crimes by Nicholas Olde.

The Julius Caesar Murder Case — A classic 1935 re-telling of the assassination by Wallace Irwin that's much more fun than the Shakespeare version.

The Koky Comics — A collection of all of the 1978-1981 Sunday and daily comic strips by Richard O'Brien and Mort Gerberg, in two volumes.

The Lady of the Terraces — 1925 missing race adventure by E. Charles Vivian.

The Lord of Terror — 1925 mystery with master-criminal, Fantômas.

The Melamare Mystery — A classic 1929 Arsene Lupin mystery by Maurice Leblanc

The Man Who Was Secrett — Epic SF stories from John Brunner

The Man Without a Planet — Science fiction tales by Richard Wilson

The N. R. De Mexico Novels — Robert Bragg, the real N.R. de Mexico, presents *Marijuana Girl, Madman on a Drum, Private Chauffeur* in one volume.

The Night Remembers — A 1991 Jack Walsh mystery from Ed Gorman.

The One After Snelling — Kickass modern noir from Richard O'Brien.

The Organ Reader — A huge compilation of just about everything published in the 1971-1972 radical bay-area newspaper, *THE ORGAN*. A coffee table book that points out the shallowness of the coffee table mindset.

The Poker Club — Three in one! Ed Gorman's ground-breaking novel, the short story it was based upon, and the screenplay of the film made from it.

The Private Journal & Diary of John H. Surratt — The memoirs of the man who conspired to assassinate President Lincoln.

The Ramble House Mapbacks — Recently revised book by Gavin L. O'Keefe with color pictures of all the Ramble House books with mapbacks.

The Secret Adventures of Sherlock Holmes — Three Sherlockian pastiches by the Brooklyn author/publisher, Gary Lovisi.

The Shadow on the House — Mark Hansom's 1934 masterpiece of horror is introduced by John Pelan.

The Sign of the Scorpion — A 1935 Edmund Snell tale of oriental evil.

The Singular Problem of the Stygian House-Boat — Two classic tales by John Kendrick Bangs about the denizens of Hades.

The Smiling Corpse — Philip Wylie and Bernard Bergman's odd 1935 novel.

The Spider: Satan's Murder Machines — A thesis about Iron Man

The Stench of Death: An Odoriferous Omnibus by Jack Moskovitz — Two complete novels and two novellas from 60's sleaze author, Jack Moskovitz.

The Story Writer and Other Stories — Classic SF from Richard Wilson

The Strange Case of the Antlered Man — 1935 dementia from Edwy Searles Brooks

The Strange Thirteen — Richard B. Gamon's odd stories about Raj India.

The Technique of the Mystery Story — Carolyn Wells' tips about writing.

The Threat of Nostalgia — A collection of his most obscure stories by Jon Breen

The Time Armada — Fox B. Holden's 1953 SF gem.

The Tongueless Horror and Other Stories — Volume One of the series of short stories from the weird pulps by Wyatt Blassingame.

The Town from Planet Five — From Richard Wilson, two SF classics, *And Then the Town Took Off* and *The Girls from Planet 5*

The Tracer of Lost Persons — From 1906, an episodic novel that became a hit radio series in the 30s. Introduced by Richard A. Lupoff.

The Trail of the Cloven Hoof — Diabolical horror from 1935 by Arlton Eadie. Introduced by John Pelan.

The Triune Man — Mindscrambling science fiction from Richard A. Lupoff.

The Unholy Goddess and Other Stories — Wyatt Blassingame's first DTP compilation

The Universal Holmes — Richard A. Lupoff's 2007 collection of five Holmesian pastiches and a recipe for giant rat stew.

The Werewolf vs the Vampire Woman — Hard to believe ultraviolence by either Arthur M. Scarm or Arthur M. Scram.

The Whistling Ancestors — A 1936 classic of weirdness by Richard E. Goddard and introduced by John Pelan.

The White Owl — A vintage thriller from Edmund Snell

The White Peril in the Far East — Sidney Lewis Gulick's 1905 indictment of the West and assurance that Japan would never attack the U.S.

The Wizard of Berner's Abbey — A 1935 horror gem written by Mark Hansom and introduced by John Pelan.

The Wonderful Wizard of Oz — by L. Frank Baum and illustrated by Gavin L. O'Keefe.

Through the Looking Glass — Lewis Carroll wrote it; Gavin L. O'Keefe illustrated it.

Time Line — Ramble House artist Gavin O'Keefe selects his most evocative art inspired by the twisted literature he reads and designs.

Tiresias — Psychotic modern horror novel by Jonathan M. Sweet.

Tortures and Towers — Two novellas of terror by Dexter Dayle.

Totah Six-Pack — Fender Tucker's six tales about Farmington in one sleek volume.

Tree of Life, Book of Death — Grania Davis' book of her life.

Triple Quest — An arty mystery from the 30s by E.R. Punshon.

Trail of the Spirit Warrior — Roger Haley's saga of life in the Indian Territories.

Two Kinds of Bad — Two 50s novels by William Ard about Danny Fontaine

Two Suns of Morcali and Other Stories — Evelyn E. Smith's SF tour-de-force

Ultra-Boiled — 23 gut-wrenching tales by our Man in Brooklyn, Gary Lovisi.

Up Front From Behind — A 2011 satire of Wall Street by James B. Kobak.

Victims & Villains — Intriguing Sherlockiana from Derham Groves.

Wade Wright Novels — *Echo of Fear, Death At Nostalgia Street, It Leads to Murder* and *Shadows' Edge*, a double book featuring *Shadows Don't Bleed* and *The Sharp Edge*.

Walter S. Masterman Novels — *The Green Toad, The Flying Beast, The Yellow Mistletoe, The Wrong Verdict, The Perjured Alibi, The Border Line, The Bloodhounds Bay, The Curse of Cantire* and *The Baddington Horror*. Masterman wrote horror and mystery, some introduced by John Pelan.

We Are the Dead and Other Stories — Volume Two in the Day Keene in the Detective Pulps series, introduced by Ed Gorman. When done, there may be 11 in the series.

Welsh Rarebit Tales — Charming stories from 1902 by Harle Oren Cummins

West Texas War and Other Western Stories — by Gary Lovisi.

What If? Volume 1, 2 and 3 — Richard A. Lupoff introduces three decades worth of SF short stories that should have won a Hugo, but didn't.

When the Batman Thirsts and Other Stories — Weird tales from Frederick C. Davis.

Whip Dodge: Man Hunter — Wesley Tallant's saga of a bounty hunter of the old West.

Win, Place and Die! — The first new mystery by Milt Ozaki in decades. The ultimate novel of 70s Reno.

Writer 1 and 2 — Richard A. Lupoff's summing up his life as writer.

You'll Die Laughing — Bruce Elliott's 1945 novel of murder at a practical joker's English countryside manor.

RAMBLE HOUSE
Fender Tucker, Prop.   Gavin L. O'Keefe, Graphics
www.ramblehouse.com   fender@ramblehouse.com
228-826-1783   10329 Sheephead Drive, Vancleave MS 39565

www.ingramcontent.com/pod-product-compliance
Lightning Source LLC
Chambersburg PA
CBHW030331020726
47493CB00004B/1233